Mad Shoes

Mad Shoes

The Adventures of
Sylvan Woods:
From Bronx Violinist
to Bulgarian Folk Dancer

Jim Gold

Full Court Press
Englewood Cliffs, New Jersey

Published in the United States of America
by Full Court Press, 601 Palisade Avenue
Englewood Cliffs, NJ 07632
www.fullcourtpressnj.com
First published by Cumberland Press in 1987

ISBN 978-1-938812-01-9
Library of Congress Catalog No. 2012943772

*Editing and Book Design by Barry Sheinkopf
for Bookshapers (www.bookshapers.com)*

Colophon by Liz Sedlack

To all my teachers

Entrance

CHAPTER ONE

First Lessons

SYLVAN WOODS WAS TIRED: Tired of books and teachers and school; tired of baggy pants that never fit; tired of eating potatoes to gain weight; tired of his mother's yelling; tired of fighting; tired of practicing . . . and he was only eleven years old. How tired would he be at twenty-five?

Outside his window, beyond the fire escape, rumbled the elevated subway. It traveled to distant places like Brooklyn and Queens. Clouds drifted across the sky above it—they too were traveling. And the sky? Where was the sky going? Limitless. Mysterious. Sky, subway, globe . . . everything was traveling. Everyone was going someplace.

Where was Sylvan Woods going?

He sat down on his bed. He was getting tired again.

His violin lay on the dresser. His grandfather had given it to him, hoping a love of music would be passed on. It was an old instrument from Amsterdam. Its scent made him think of old Dutch paintings, wharves of Amsterdam harbors, and merchant ships of historic Holland—ruler of the seas.

He lay on his back, imagining the canals of Holland projected across the ceiling. Holland seemed so peaceful. He saw Rubens put aside his easel and lie down under a tree. Soon the artist was asleep.

"Sylvan, why aren't you practicing?"

He sat up. "I was practicing, Ma, but—"

"No more 'buts.' " His mother walked into the room and stood in front of him, arms akimbo. "Get on your feet. You can't practice lying down. Why do you lie in bed every time you practice? That's no way to learn."

"I was thinking about the music."

"Never mind that. Save the thinking for later. Your job is to practice."

Sylvan defended himself: "Sam says it's good to think."

"You weren't thinking. You were daydreaming again!" His mother's tone softened. "Sylvan, please practice. I want to be proud of you at your next lesson."

Sylvan took his violin out of the case, tucked it under his chin, and drew the bow. Grating noises filled the room.

That's better," his mother said. "I'll shut the door so you won't be disturbed."

Although Sylvan liked music, violin lessons with Sam Ferdinand made him nervous. Was it fear of playing poorly and disappointing his teacher? Or was it Sam himself?

Sam Ferdinand was fifty years old. He walked with a stoop that made him look shorter than his stocky five feet eight. He wore pin-striped suits and combed every hair on his head exactly in place. In a bag hanging from his violin case he carried soap, a washcloth, a comb, Kleenex, and shoe polish—ammunition in his fight against dirt. He also had a rag he snapped at students when they missed a note.

Sam liked to sit back in his chair after a lesson and philosophize. During these moments he would pick his nose, concentrating his attention on his right nostril. When Sam felt good, his nostrils flared up bright red.

Sam Ferdinand had his own approach to teaching, believing in one right way and many wrong ways of playing. The right way was easy to define: It was his way.

Sylvan's lessons were given on Wednesday afternoon at five o'-clock—often in the middle of a baseball, football, or basketball game—depending on the season.

"Hi, Sam," Sylvan exclaimed breathlessly as he raced into the bathroom to wash. "I'll be right there."

When he entered his room, Sam was sitting on a chair tuning the violin. "I'm glad you washed, Sylvan," he said, looking up from the chin rest. "Always wash your hands before you play. Unclean hands make unclean music." He stopped tuning, put down the violin, and began leafing through the Wohlfahrt Studies. Then he lectured: "You know what happened to Hard-Handed Harry and his Hairy Violin. Harry never washed before playing. Soon the dirt on his hands got so hard it ruined his music. The New York Fire Department hired him to play at burning buildings to hurry people out." At this, Sam moved closer to Sylvan. "Now, Harry had a style, but I would never call him an artist. In order to create fine art, the first step is clean hands. All great composers were clean. Beethoven was the cleanest of all."

"I like that story, Sam." Sylvan turned up his soap-scrubbed hands for examination. "How do you like these?"

Sam's bushy eyebrows narrowed; he explored every fold of skin, sniffing the palms and fingers. "Not bad at all."

"Sam?"

"Yes?"

"What's on your hands?"

Sam studied his palm. "Ink," he answered. "It's because I am a teacher and my calling is to spread the art of music. Jesus had cuts on his hands; music teachers have ink on theirs. . . . But enough of this talk. Let me hear you play."

Sylvan raised the violin to his chin and played a C scale. Sam's face turned pale. "Stop!" he howled. "It's a violin, not a baseball bat. Press lightly on the strings . . . gently . . . caress them." He held Sylvan's wrist and guided the bow across the strings.

At the end of the lesson, Sam looked pleased. "Much better," he said, leaning back in satisfaction. "Your playing has improved. But you still have a long way to go. You play the Wohlfahrt too gently now. Also, the Kreutzer Study is weak." He straightened in his chair. "Practice to make those notes tough—especially the ones on the G and D strings. I want meat on them; I want Wohlfahrt and Kreutzer to rise from their graves when they hear your mighty notes. I myself want to hear your mighty notes." Sam pushed the violin back under Sylvan's chin. "Play them for me, Sylvan. Play them!"

Sylvan played the first two measures of the Kreutzer Study. The D string snapped.

Sam slumped back in his chair. He looked sadly at the ceiling. "He's telling me something," he groaned. "He's telling me something."

"Who is telling you something?" Sylvan asked, lowering his violin.

Sam's eyes were fixed on a crack in the ceiling. "The Lord of Music is speaking to me again. He is telling me my pupils cannot play the mighty notes. He is telling me I have failed." Then, without warning, he sprang from his chair. "No, no," he shouted, stamping the floor. "It's not me. The Lord of Music is on my side!" He glared at Sylvan. "It's you, you!"

"Me?"

"Yes, you!" Sam pointed his finger at Sylvan. "But I won't let it happen this time. I won't let you ruin me. You'll practice, by God. You'll practice until the trees bend to hear you. I'll make something out of you, you wait and see."

"Yes, sir, I'm sure you will." Sylvan glanced at Sam's wristwatch, hoping the lesson would end soon.

Sam wiped his forehead with a handkerchief. "I'm too upset to continue. For next week, keep practicing the Kreutzer. I've got some thinking to do about you." He looked around the room. "I want pictures of Kreisler, Heifetz, and Stern on these walls. And I want records of violin concertos in that corner instead of a baseball bat."

Sam packed his briefcase. "Some day you'll thank me for the hours you've spent practicing here," he warned as he left the room.

Sylvan closed the door behind him. Glancing at the baseball heroes on his wall, he thought he saw Joe DiMaggio, in center field, catching a violin.

Mrs. Woods had just finished squeezing avocados and blue cheese into her salad dressing when she met Sam in the hallway. "A good lesson," Sam reassured her, tucking his violin under his arm. "Sylvan shows promise."

"I'm glad to hear that, Mr. Ferdinand," she said, wiping her hands on her apron. "He's a good boy, even though he daydreams a lot."

Sam sniffed the potatoes and chopped meat cooking on the stove. "Dreams are an important part of art," he remarked. "All creative people daydream."

"That's nice."

"Yes, Mrs. Woods, without our dreams we would be barren and empty."

"Then you think Sylvan's daydreaming isn't so bad?"

"It's good to dream."

Sylvan's mother wiped her hands again. "I suppose so," she sighed. "He's really a good boy even though I still think he daydreams too much. . . . And then, of course, there are his attacks."

Sam looked surprised. "Attacks?"

Mrs. Woods reached for her pocketbook. She pulled out four dollars and handed them to Sam. "We don't know what causes them," she said. "Sylvan has been to several doctors. They can't figure it out either."

Sam leaned forward. "What kind of attacks are these?"

"Frightening ones. They always come unexpectedly—and for no apparent reason."

"Go on, go on."

Mrs. Woods squeezed her apron. "When Sylvan has an attack, he'll yell or slap himself. He laughs; he cries. Sometimes he dances."

Sam shook his head. "That is strange."

"Last Saturday we had the family over for dinner," Mrs. Woods went on. "Sylvan sat next to his uncle. Everyone was eating when suddenly he started stamping on the floor. The whole table shook. I yelled, 'Sylvan, stop that!' But he went right on doing it." Mrs. Woods wrung her hands in despair. "It's not my fault; it's not my fault!"

"Of course it's not," Sam reassured her. "The Lord of Music works in mysterious ways. Go on."

Mrs. Woods sighed. "He stamped and slapped himself. His uncle tried holding him down, but Sylvan just giggled until the roast beef came out of his mouth. It was disgusting. Then he blinked, sat perfectly still, and began eating again as if nothing had happened."

Sam asked, "Could it be epilepsy?"

"No. It's not that. The boy has been tested for everything from epilepsy to syphilis; they even x-rayed his brain for a tumor. No, Sylvan is in perfect health. The doctors can't figure it out."

Sam opened the door. "I've got another lesson," he said, "but I'm going to give these attacks a lot of thought. The human mind is a mysterious place."

Mrs. Woods agreed. "Especially Sylvan's mind."

CHAPTER TWO

Preparation

S O SYLVAN BEGAN TO practice. During the next five years, his life changed. Outdoor sports gave way to indoor study. Afternoons and weekends he spent in his room making music.

As he improved, and the habit of daily practice became stronger, he began enjoying the violin. Baseball, basketball, radio programs, football, pranks, and other interests slipped away. Practicing became his way of life. In school he daydreamed about music. He imagined the violin in his hand while teachers lectured on math, science, and history. He didn't care why George Washington crossed the Delaware, or about the effects of gravity on the moon and ocean waves, or about Dante's view of purgatory. These things were fine— for other people. He wanted to be left alone, to let his mind wander. . . . And it kept wandering back to the violin.

By age fifteen he was working on more advanced pieces. After warming up with scales and arpeggios, he took apart the difficult passages in the Bruch Concerto, the Mendelssohn Concerto, burrowed through Bach partitas and Lalo's *Symphonie Espagnole*, playing them over and over until he had mastered each note. Sam taught him how to make a *crescendo*, a *diminuendo*, a dramatic contrast between a *forte* and a *piano* passage. These expressive techniques captured his imagination. Sam no longer had to tell him to work at it. In fact, Sam often had to slow him down.

Sometimes when he played, he'd feel a wonderful rush of energy. It moved like electricity—first in his hands, then to his arms, his back, and down to his legs. His fingers flew faster and faster, almost out of control. His bow danced on the strings. He'd sway with the music. He'd laugh, cry, shout, and stamp on the floor. Then he'd start to dance! Gliding, then leaping across the room, violin under his chin, bow bouncing from bridge to fingerboard, he sang orchestral accompaniments to the concertos he played. And if a concerto or *étude* had no accompaniment, he'd make one up, humming a figured bass or giving old Wohlfahrt an oriental flavor by singing in fourths.

He loved these wild moments in his room. They didn't come often, and they didn't last long, but when they came, they were great! He'd remember them for days. Sylvan suspected that Beethoven must have had the same wild times, and Mozart, and Mendelssohn, too. All composers had visits. He wanted more of them. He wanted to preserve them. But how could he? They were so spontaneous, so ephemeral. The energy came to you suddenly, as a gift, then left just as quickly. Sylvan loved the wonder of it.

It was a good thing his door was closed during these visits from the Lord of Music. If his mother or father had ever seen him dancing around his room, or stamping on the floor and shouting, they would have called the doctor again. His parents would never understand. What adult could know what he was talking about? Or even kids his age, for that matter.

Sam was pleased with Sylvan's progress. "None of my students work as hard as you do," he said one afternoon at the end of a lesson. "I'm proud of you. And you should be proud of yourself."

He put his hand on Sylvan's shoulder. "Now for the big surprise. Every December, when the Bronx Symphonette gives a concert in Addington Hall, they invite a young musician to perform with them. The conductor, Vladimir Gussman, is a good friend of mine. I had lunch with him yesterday and told him about you." Sam smiled. "He wants you to audition for him. If you pass, you'll be the soloist at the Christmas concert."

Sam sat back. "Now what do you think of that?"

"It's scary," Sylvan answered slowly. "I've never played with an orchestra before—and in front of all those people. It's scary."

Sam reassured him. "Sure it's scary. Every artist is scared. You wouldn't be an artist if you weren't scared."

"Really?"

"Of course. Fear is a great asset. All artists must learn to deal with it—and believe me, all artists are scared. Did you know that Brahms was afraid his First Symphony would be a failure; Toscanini was afraid whenever he conducted; and Horowitz is petrified before he goes on stage." Sam paused. Sylvan was listening carefully. "But fear is also good," Sam went on. "Fear can motivate you; it can give you energy. Then you can use that energy to study more, to practice harder. Soon you'll find your fears dissolving and turning into excitement."

Sylvan looked dubious. "I hope you're right."

"Do you doubt me, young man? Of course I'm right. I know this business inside out. And I know fear very well. Do you know why? Because not a day goes by without my stomach churning with worry. But I keep going. I've learned to work with it. I've learned to make fear my friend."

"I hope I can do that some day," Sylvan said wistfully. Sam stroked his chin. "You will," he replied. "But it takes time and practice. You have ability and talent. Hopefully, you'll surpass me." He put his violin in its case and snapped it shut. "I've arranged your audition for next Thursday at Gussman's apartment. I'll leave the address with your mother."

Thursday afternoon, Sylvan stood before a brownstone on Ninety-sixth Street. A uniformed doorman opened the door a crack. "What do you want?" he demanded.

Sylvan's throat was dry. "Mr. Gussman's," he whispered nervously.

The man pushed the door open further. "What?" he asked, jangling his keys on his belt. "Speak up."

"G-G-Guss—"

"Gooseman. Apartment 3A. Take the elevator to your right."

Sylvan stepped out on the third floor. He pressed Gussman's bell. The door opened and a woman stuck her head out. "Yes?" she croaked.

". . . Er . . . I'm Sylvan Woods."

The woman smiled mirthlessly. "Come in."

They walked down a hallway to the living room. Sylvan looked around. The walls were papered in gray; piles of music, records, books, and papers were scattered over a Steinway Grand that dominated the generous space. Light filtered through the tall rectangular window overlooking Ninety-sixth Street—it looked as if it hadn't been cleaned for years. As Sylvan's eyes adjusted to the semi-darkness, he noticed an arm-chair covered in black velvet. Something unusual about the armchair made him focus on it. A man was sitting there, almost invisible—camouflaged by his black jacket, black shirt and tie, black pants, black shoes and socks, black hair. He sat motionless against the black background of the arm-chair. A white face peered out of the blackness. It was Vladimir Gussman.

Sylvan stepped forward. "Hello, Mr. Gussman. I'm Sylvan

Woods."

"I know, I know," Gussman answered. "I have been waiting for you."

"I didn't mean to keep you waiting."

"Don't worry," Gussman replied in his thick Russian accent. "I like to wait." He turned towards the dining room. "Natasha! Bring *chai*." His wife entered, set a tray in front of Gussman, and tiptoed out.

Gussman poured some tea. He fixed his eyes on Sylvan. "Play!" he commanded.

Sylvan took out his violin. His fingers slipped as he tightened the bow. Then he played a Mozart sonata, two Bach partitas, and part of the Bruch Concerto.

Gussman sipped his tea. "Interesting," he commented. "Woods, you play with much feeling. I like Mozart sonatas. You dance when you play. I like it." He paused to reflect. "You like basketball?"

"Why . . . er . . . yes."

"Good!" Gussman became animated. His arms wove hook-shots and set-shots in the air. "I like Harlem Globetrotters," he said proudly. Then he told Sylvan about his research in sports history, his training as a sprinter in Moscow, and his new love of American basketball.

Finally, Gussman's lips curled into a smile. "Woods, I like your playing. You like basketball. I like you. I want you for concert."

"Thank you, Mr. Gussman." The words rushed out of Sylvan's mouth again, "Thank you!"

"*Nichevo*. Nothing." Gussman reached into his pocket and pulled out a ticket. "For game tonight," he said, handing it to Sylvan. "New York against Milwaukee in Madison Square Garden."

"Wonderful!" Sam exclaimed when he heard about the audition. "What an honor! What a goal!"

"Do you think playing basketball had anything to do with it?" Sylvan asked.

"No." Sam was emphatic. "It was your violin playing—although playing basketball never hurts. Knowing a sport is always good. Felix Mendelssohn liked hiking. In fact, I think you should play his concerto at the concert.

"The Mendelssohn Concerto?"

"Only the first movement. It's tough, but you can do it. You know most of it already. All the notes are fingered; you know which ones to accent; the triplets and double stops in section A are good, and you play the cadenza well. Your main weakness is too much rubato-—you take too many liberties with the tempo. The Romantics loved rubato. But performers in those days had more freedom than we do. They even added notes and improvised. Still, too much freedom destroys the character of the music." Sam put the concerto on the music stand and opened to page one. "We have three months to refine this. You're going to learn not just how to play Mendelssohn, but how to perform him.

Sam pointed to the opening measures. "The first thing to do is memorize every note. My method is to play a passage fifteen times one day, eight times the next day, and four times the next. The key is: Play the sections you are memorizing every day. That way, you'll know this concerto so well you can read the New York Times while playing it or even carry on a conversation with me. By using this method, I am still able to remember pieces from my childhood, even though I haven't played them for years."

Sylvan tried the "Ferdinand" method, but somehow it didn't work for him. Once he started playing, he found it hard to stop. Repeating passages over and over again seemed mechanical and boring. Haunted by the beautiful melodies, he'd just play the first movement from beginning to end. By playing it many times, it slowly became part of him. As for Sam's comment on Sylvan's approach: "I think it's lousy, but if it works, use it."

"We're in good shape," Sam said after five weeks. "You've memorized the concerto. Now it's time for mental preparation. Learn everything about Mendelssohn's life. How did he sleep? What did he eat? What books did he read? How did he feel taking piano lessons from his mother? What was life like in Berlin and Leipzig? And what about his journeys to England and Scotland, or his delicate health? These questions are important, because to perform Mendelssohn, you must learn to think and feel like Mendelssohn. You must become Mendelssohn! Then, when you play his concerto, you'll be playing your concerto."

Sylvan spent many hours in the library learning about his new hero. Mendelssohn's achievements were fantastic; he could do almost anything. He was one of the finest pianists of his time and a great conductor and organist, had a perfect ear and marvelous memory, was well read, liked poetry and philosophy, painted well. Sylvan took long walks and tried to see the world through the composer's eyes. He practiced being Mendelssohn.

"When you make your debut, bearing will be important," Sam said one afternoon. "I'm going to show you how to bow." Sam taught Sylvan to stand erect, walk with pride, put both feet together, look straight into the audience, part his lips in a smile, and bow forwards from the waist. During the following weeks, he practiced at supermarkets and at school. The results amazed him—check-out clerks congratulated him for being such a polite young man; teachers complimented him on his manners.

One week before the concert, Sam sat opposite Sylvan and observed, "A job well done. Everything is in order. The Mendelssohn has become a part of you. Added to this, you bow beautifully and can walk on stage with dignity and grace.

There's not much more I can teach you for this performance. All we can do now is hope for the gift."

"The gift?" Sylvan asked.

"Inspiration, revelation, gift, or whatever," Sam explained. "It's hard to describe. No one knows how to make it happen. But when it happens, when you get the gift, you know it. And the audience knows it, too. It's a great moment. Suddenly, you realize your potential—what you can do if you give everything you've got."

Sam rose from his chair and closed his violin case. "Think about that, Sylvan, he said.

Sylvan thought about it all week.

CHAPTER THREE

The Concert

I T WAS A WINTRY December evening when Sylvan arrived at Addington Hall, a stately building constructed in the Greek Revival style of the late nineteenth century. Although an hour before showtime, most of the seats in the auditorium were already taken. He hurried down the aisle, past the reprints of Velásquez and El Greco hanging on the walls, and glanced at the domed ceiling above the orchestra. Behind him someone whispered, "There he is; there's the soloist."

Sylvan's stomach rumbled. He had never been so nervous before. Parents, relatives, friends, teachers, critics, everyone would be sitting in that audience watching and listening to him.

The orchestra musicians were warming up on stage. Their tuxedos, white shirts, bow ties, and bald heads shone under the lights. No one smiled. Sylvan knew they meant business. Gussman appeared in the wings, hurried down the stairs, greeted Sylvan, and led him backstage. "You look wonderful," he exclaimed. "I like tuxedo and white shirt." He faced the audience and swept his hand theatrically before him. "They will love you. And they will love me. A perfect combination!"

Sylvan gulped, squeezed the violin case under his arm, and followed Gussman backstage.

He spent most of the next hour on the toilet while the orchestra warmed up with scales, arpeggios, and short passages from the score.

At 8:30 the lights dimmed. Applause greeted Vladimir Gussman. He walked proudly across the stage, bowed, pulled his baton out of his vest pocket, and stepped to the podium. You could tell he had been a runner by the way he conducted Mozart's Jupiter Symphony. Although he held his baton in his right hand, both arms moved back and forth like pistons racing along with the rhythm of the music. The musicians could follow either hand with equal ease.

As Mozart was being performed onstage, Sylvan took out his violin and started warming up.

Sam came backstage. "Sorry I'm late," he said, throwing his coat over a chair. He saw the pleading look in Sylvan's eyes. "Don't worry. Relax. You can do it. You know this concerto so well, you can perform it in your sleep."

Sylvan's fingers slid off the neck as he played an arpeggio; his bow skipped on the strings. "Who's worried?" he answered, as his bow popped out of his hand and fell on the floor. Only the greatest restraint kept him from escaping through the fire exit.

The Jupiter Symphony was followed by a ten-minute intermission, after which Gussman again climbed to the podium. He leafed through the score while the orchestra tuned up. Then he raised his hands. The orchestra and audience became quiet. With a nod of his head, Gussman signaled for Sylvan to make his entrance.

Sylvan's knees felt like buckling as he walked across the stage. At the first violin, he turned, faced the audience, and put his feet together. His lips parted in a sickly smile as he bowed stiffly from the waist. Then he unlocked his teeth and turned to face his conductor.

Gussman winked at him and lifted his baton. The melodic opening of Mendelssohn's Violin Concerto sounded through the hall. Sylvan got the violin under his chin just in time to start his solo. Although the score said "Molto Appassionato," he had no "appassionato" in him. In fact, his mind went blank. A few mousy notes squeaked out of his violin. His bow bounced all over the strings, destroying the flow of the opening measures. Luckily, some notes were in place, but that was about it. Down bows turned into up bows, accented notes were left out, and new ones put in their place. When the triplets in section A arrived, he substituted rests in their place. Whole measures disappeared. Yet, when his first solo ended and the score called for silence, he inserted all the double stops, triplets, and arpeggios he had previously left out.

Gussman, gritting his teeth, kept conducting with iron determination, but his knuckles were turning blue around his baton.

Suddenly, thanks to Sylvan's training—the countless hours of repetition—his fingers and bow began to move automatically. Gradually, he began to relax. His fingers performed what they had been trained to perform. He played with poise, though his shirt was drenched with sweat.

From that point on, he didn't miss a note. Soon he was totally immersed in the concerto. His solo soared above the orchestra's accompaniment. Out of the corner of his eye, he saw Gussman smiling happily to himself. Sylvan made his violin speak, cry out, sing; cascading arpeggios and dramatic runs poured from his heart into the music. He forgot the audience as memories of Mendelssohn flooded his mind. Swept along, he began humming. Then he sang softly to himself. His feet tapped as he swayed from side-to-side.

Sylvan entered the nineteenth century. He was performing in Leipzig before barons and aristocrats, before Mendelssohn's fans, his friends and musical world.

Having forgotten about the audience, Sylvan also began to forget about Gussman's happy smile.

When he came to the cadenza, the orchestra stopped playing. This was Sylvan's solo. Mendelssohn had written it for the performer to show his stuff, and to show it *ad libitum*. Sylvan attacked the opening note of the cadenza with such force his bow almost broke. He raced through the next few measures before arriving at the *fermata* on low B. Most musicians held that *fermata* twice as long as written. But Sylvan held it so long, the orchestra and audience thought he had either fallen asleep or was in a trance. Gussman signaled the first violinist to tap Sylvan's shoulder. The young soloist then left the low B only to play an ascending arpeggio and arrive at the high B. He held that *fermata* even longer.

"Move on, Sylvan!" Gussman muttered. Nothing happened, so he poked Sylvan in the ribs with his baton.

Then it started. Sylvan descended from the high B, skipped eight measures, and started trilling. He trilled on A; he trilled on C; he trilled on E. He trilled on A and E together, pounding his fingers on the fingerboard with such intensity and breathtaking speed that he made Tartini's *Devil's Trill Sonata* seem like a kindergarten warm-up exercise. Then he began adding "new" notes to the cadenza, notes Mendelssohn never dreamed of. Gussman winced, but let the "mistakes" go, thinking—hoping—that Sylvan was simply nervous or had forgotten the original score. He felt better when Sylvan, after bowing wildly on a descending arpeggio and playing diminuendo and piano where the music was clearly marked *accellerando* and forte, arrived at the famous *spiccato* bowing passage—the ending of the cadenza. It was here that the orchestra rejoined him.

Gussman lifted his baton and brought his musicians in gracefully. The opening measures were smooth and lovely. Sylvan played all the written notes correctly—in tempo and in tune.

But then Gussman heard something strange. For a moment, the music Sylvan was playing didn't sound like Mendelssohn at all.

He was right. Sylvan wasn't playing Mendelssohn. He was playing the Beethoven Concerto! Gussman didn't know what to do. He was about to stop the orchestra when Sylvan wandered back to the score.

Relieved, Gussman relaxed. But Sylvan suddenly switched again—this time to a Bach *partita*. He jumped to a Mozart sonata before playing parts of Lalo's *Symphonie Espagnole*. The audience didn't know what to make of it. Some sat with puzzled expressions; others shifted uneasily in their seats. Whispering began to fill the hall.

"What's going on here?" asked a man in the fourth row as Sylvan started to dance.

"Isadora Duncan's choreography," answered the ballerina behind him.

"Theater of the absurd," put in the music critic from the *Riverdale Gazette*.

Yes, the audience knew something unusual was happening.

But Sylvan was no longer aware of the audience. He stamped his foot; he shook and twisted his hips; his dancing got wilder. "Whahooooo! *Haaaaiiiiiiup!*" he cried, kicking his legs high in the air and hopping around the podium. He forgot who he was. He forgot where he was.

He was having an attack.

At first, the other musicians played along, hoping for the best.

Now, however, they were totally confused. They would have ground to a halt, but Gussman spurred them on, though he didn't know where he was going either. He had never heard such music before. Sylvan was no longer playing Bach, Beethoven, Mendelssohn, or anyone else. No, he was improvising!

The orchestra kept doggedly playing the Mendelssohn Concerto. Strangely, Sylvan's improvised melodies blended perfectly with the orchestral accompaniment. Learning to think and feel like Mendelssohn had obviously had its effect.

The orchestra came to the end of the concerto. But Sylvan didn't! His playing resounded above Gussman's cries of "Stop! Stop!" Gussman was about to drag him off when the lad suddenly stopped playing, put the violin under his arm, bowed to the audience, and walked off the stage.

The silence was broken by the sound of Mrs. Woods sobbing in the first row.

Sam leaped out of his seat. "Bravo, Bravo!" He hugged Mrs. Woods, but it only made her sob louder.

"I enjoyed that one," Mr. Woods said, lifting his accountant's pencil from the figures he had been adding on the program.

Scattered applause could be heard in the balcony; a woman in an aisle seat began sobbing; high-pitched giggles rose from the back row.

"What's going on here?" repeated the man in the fourth row.

Gussman remained dumbfounded while the audience clapped and wept. A Juilliard student began dancing in the aisles.

Finally, Gussman signaled his orchestra to rise. He turned to the audience, bowed, and stepped down from the podium. The cheers were getting louder as he walked off the stage.

Pandemonium had broken loose in the auditorium when Gussman arrived at his dressing room. Screams, bellows, howls of laughter, applause, sporadic hissing, giggles, booing, crying; it sounded like the Bronx Zoo in summer. Torn between depression and rage, he slammed the door so hard, the mirror on the wall shook. He pulled off his jacket and was about to throw it over the armchair when he noticed someone sitting in it. It was Sylvan. Gussman nearly kicked him, but something about the boy's expression made him stop. Sylvan was leaning back in the armchair, one leg sprawled over its side. He looked relaxed. There was a smile on his face.

CHAPTER FOUR

After the Concert

THE MORNING AFTER THE concert, the phone rang constantly. Relatives, friends, teachers, neighbors called to congratulate Sylvan. Some favorable reviews appeared in the local papers.

Sylvan was so happy with the results of his concert that for weeks he could think of nothing else. Questions about his future filled his mind. Should he concertize? Should he follow Mendelssohn's footsteps and compose?

Sylvan's parents were also confused about his direction. Obviously, their son had talent—but so did thousands of others. The field of music was so competitive, earning a living in it so precarious. . . . Should he keep it as a hobby, they asked themselves, or push ahead to make it his career?

A few weeks later, they invited Sam into the living room for a short discussion about Sylvan's future. Sam sat in front of the coffee table, filled his glass with orange juice, and listened.

"It's up to Sylvan," Mr. Woods said, sitting up on the sofa.

"Of course it's up to him," Mrs. Woods agreed. "I want my son to be happy. I want him to do what he wants. But so many have tried and failed—even geniuses. What chance does he have?"

Sam came up with an idea. "Sylvan will be graduating high school in three months. Why not let him spend a year abroad, in France, and continue his studies there."

"Oh, no," Mrs. Woods protested. "Sylvan's not going all the way to France. He's too young for that."

Sam placed his hand on Mrs. Woods' wrist. "Don't worry," he coaxed. "He could study in Paris with Madame Lefebre. I know her from the Conservatory. She takes a personal interest in all her students. She's like a mother to them."

"Sylvan doesn't need another mother," Mrs. Woods replied somewhat distantly. "Besides, he doesn't speak French."

"Sylvan is ready," Sam insisted. "He's ready to strike out on his own."

"He may be ready," Mrs. Woods hissed, "but I'm not."

"Martha, it's Sylvan's life," Mr. Woods broke in. "Let him decide."

"You stay out of this, Harry! It's none of your business!"

"Calm down, Mrs. Woods." Sam took her by the elbow and walked her around the living room. When they passed the bookshelf, he pulled down a book on French art, leafed through it, then pulled down another, a well-illustrated volume on woodworking and interior designs of the 18th century. "Relax," he said. "A year abroad will be good for Sylvan."

"A year!"

"Mrs. Woods, this is just what Sylvan needs for his emotional and intellectual growth. And Madame Lefebre is a marvelous teacher. Her students practice and compose in her home during the day. Evenings they play chamber music or go to a concert. Weekends are often spent at the Louvre. Madame Lefebre is also an art expert."

Mrs. Woods' voice softened. "I don't know. . . . An art expert?"

"Yes. Her specialty is Louis XIV furniture."

"Louis XIV? Why, Sylvan wrote a report on Louis XIV in eighth grade."

"Believe me, Mrs. Woods, Madame Lefebre would be the perfect teacher for Sylvan."

"I love Louis XIV furniture."

"It's wonderful furniture." Sam walked Mrs. Woods around the living room again. "You'll be glad," he told her. "It's an ideal way for Sylvan to spend the year."

Mrs. Woods nodded. Mr. Woods did, too. They called Sylvan in. He loved the idea—foreign country, new language, travel and adventure, a chance to get away from home—exciting images filled his mind.

A new chapter in his life was beginning.

CHAPTER FIVE

France

SYLVAN HAD STUDIED FRENCH in high school and had received fine marks from his teacher. But he couldn't really speak French. After meeting five times a week for two years in high school French classes, "A"'s on Madame Poignard's tricky quizzes, a senior paper on the minuet and dance movements of Louis XIV, hours of self-hypnosis through the repetition of irregular verbs, nouns, adjectives, and reflexives, and study sessions with his mother which he called "flagellation through conjugation," when it came to an actual conversation with a French person, he couldn't understand a word.

Coming off the boat at Le Havre, he became aware of this linguistic void with startling suddenness when he asked the passport official which train went to Paris. The official's answer came so fast—the French nasals and gutturals springing from his mouth with such speed—that Sylvan could only respond with a limp *oui*. But he understood immediately when the official *pointed* to a train waiting on the tracks nearby. Sylvan boarded it and hoped it was going to Paris.

Once there, he visited book stores and bakeries on the Rive

Gauche, explored cobblestone streets and back alleys, stopped to eat in crowded cafes. Each day he spoke with Parisians on the street, in stores, or while they stood in *pissoires*, and practiced his miserable French on them. Using his limited vocabulary with limited skill, he managed to confuse some and make others laugh by asking questions with misplaced accents and following these with meaningless comments completely out of context.

"*Bonjour, ami. Comment allez le chien s'il vous plait. Oui, il fait beau, non? J'aime Paris, mais ou est la maison? Demain je suis fatigue. Louis XIV était Roi de France.*"

After he had delivered this babble, the Parisians he met answered with machine-gun speed; and, as Sylvan stood by dazed, they walked away with satisfied looks on their faces.

He hoped to become more fluent before his first meeting with Madame Lefebre.

It was a clear September day when Sylvan made his first visit to her chateau on the outskirts of Paris. A student aide opened the gate and led him into the courtyard. Once inside, Sylvan could see the crenelations along the northern wall flanked by two square turrets. A musical fortress. He felt well-protected.

His heels clicked in the stone hallway as they passed ornate furniture and tapestries before arriving in a spacious living room with walls covered in velvet. Paintings by Watteau and Fragonard decorated the walls. Two windows overlooked a garden with a fishpond, flowers, sculpted paths, and bushes pruned in the shape of arrowheads. A scent of roses filled the air. Sitting at one of the grand pianos in front of the fireplace was a beautiful woman whose black, braided hair fell in knots over her left shoulder. Her dark eyes searched Sylvan's face.

He tried not to stare at her full breasts, and concentrated instead on her lovely mouth.

She smiled. "*Entrez, s'il vous plait.*"

Sylvan kept staring.

"Please, come in." She spoke English with a delicious French accent. Sylvan's first step into the room seemed like his first step into paradise.

"I am Madame Lefebre," she said, rising from the piano and walking toward him. "You are Sylvan Woods, *non*?" Sylvan nodded.

"Come, sit with me." She took him by the arm and led him to the piano bench. "Here, next to me," she insisted, patting the treble side of the bench with her right hand.

Sylvan's gangly body somehow squeezed between the bench and piano keys.

"Let us begin." Madame Lefebre's voice sang to him; her perfume was making him dizzy. "Play something for me, please."

Sylvan placed his hands on the black and white keys and pressed hard. Madame Lefebre paled. "Is that an original sound?" she asked hopefully. "An original composition?"

Sylvan shook his head.

She scowled. "Not a work of a master?" She looked puzzled. "It is your *interpretation* of a master's work? Perhaps a Beethoven sonata?"

Again, Sylvan shook his head.

"What is it then?"

"A mistake."

"Mistake?"

"Yes. I don't play piano."

"*Non?*" She looked baffled.

"I play violin."

She stood up. "How can you call yourself a musician and not play piano?" she asked flatly. Her hands fluttered in the air, looking for direction. "Yes, of course, you play violin . . . or viola, or bassoon, or no matter what. *Mon Dieu,* everybody plays something, no matter how insignificant the instrument may be. But it is impossible to understand music, impossible to understand composition, harmony, theory, dynamics . . . it is . . . it is impossible to understand *anything* unless you play piano." She shook her head sadly. "How could Sam have sent you to me without first learning piano?"

"I'm sorry I can't play piano," Sylvan said, "but I could learn."

"You could, eh? Who would teach you?"

Sylvan thought a moment. "You could teach me."

"Me? Why, I have no time for this! I teach *composition,* not the mere technique of moving fingers across the keys."

She stepped from the piano bench and walked towards the fireplace, digging her sharp heels into the rug. Suddenly, she stopped. "Why not?" she thought aloud. "I could teach him my way." She chuckled softly. "My *way.*" She turned to Sylvan, studied him at a distance, then moved closer. "Very well. I will teach you. Put your hands on the piano. . . . Now play."

"But I don't know how to play," Sylvan protested.

"That is not important. Play."

Cautiously, he pressed a white key, then a black. They felt hard, brittle. He played black and white keys together, moving less hesitantly up and down the keyboard.

Madame Lefebre sat down on a *fauteuil* with *cabriole* legs. Her fingers brushed slowly over its upholstered arms as she sat in silence and waited.

Interpreting her silence as approval, Sylvan began playing with more confidence. At first, he used only his finger tips; but as he became more involved, he started rolling his hands across the keys instead. From rolling, he advanced to light karate chops on the white keys and hammering his fist on the black. He flattened his palm, stretched his fingers, and pressed down twenty-three notes at once. Soon he was pushing the pedals and pounding the piano in every which way, making all kinds of strange sounds.

Fifteen minutes passed. Finally, she told him to stop. "That is the way I teach," she said. "Go home and practice."

Sylvan pushed his bench away from the keyboard. "But you haven't taught me anything," he objected.

"What? Oh, you stupid! You have already learned more from me than in all your years of study."

"I have?"

"Oui! But you do not realize it yet. But you will." She stood up and pointed to the door. "Now go home and practice."

During the following weeks the pattern of each lesson was the same; Sylvan would sit down at the piano and play whatever came to mind. Madame Lefebre never said a word. She listened—carefully. At the end of each lesson she said, "Go home and practice."

Sylvan couldn't understand what she was listening to. But, as the weeks passed, he began enjoying the lessons more and more. Practicing and playing seemed so easy. Whatever he played was good; whatever he felt was good; whatever he did was good. Madame Lefebre heard it all with equanimity. She didn't judge. She only listened . . . and accepted.

Sylvan also enjoyed playing the piano when she sat on the bench next to him because whenever he hit the high notes, his elbows brushed against her full breasts. He soon found himself playing many more high notes than low notes during his improvisations. He also learned to linger on each note and make a dreamy soulful expression.

One day he lingered so long she stopped him. "Your playing has too many high notes," she said, rising from the piano bench.

"You need to use a wider range on the keyboard." Then she walked over to the bass side of the piano and sat next to him. It was a turning point in his training.

After three months of lessons, Sylvan said, "I think I've been making progress on the piano, Madame Lefebre. But I came to France to study composition. When will I learn how to compose music?"

"You *are* learning," she answered. "You have been learning from the moment you came. Every lesson with me is a lesson in composition. Composition means: To discover your voice. You are discovering it."

"Do you like my voice?"

"Do I like it?" she asked. "It does not matter whether I like your voice; it does not matter whether *you* like your voice. It only matters that you *discover your voice,* and are true to it."

"I like your voice, Madame Lefebre."

"You have never heard my voice."

"I hear it at every lesson," he breathed.

She understood. "That is not the voice I am talking about," she replied, gently putting her hand on Sylvan's shoulder. "But I am glad you like my *other* voice."

During that lesson, Sylvan's improvisations improved; he played with a new richness and fluidity.

One day she led him past her boudoir and into a lavishly decorated bed-chamber. A monumental Louis XIV bed stood in the center of the floor; its posts supported a velvet canopy with golden gadroons and orange and green tassels hanging from its scalloped borders. The curtains enclosing the bed were covered with embroidery. To the right stood an overstuffed sofa sprinkled with pillows.

Madame Lefebre sat down on the sofa. "Here one can hear my *other* voice," she whispered. Her delicate feet sank into the carpet as she glided towards the mirror whose surface reflected the light of the garden. Resting her elbow on the commode and stroking its satinwood marquetry with sensual slowness, she gazed at Sylvan.

They sat down on the sofa. Her hands touched his face, fingertips stopping gently on his lips. Her dark eyes commanded him as she looked right into his soul.

Sylvan's stomach moved in all directions.

Her student didn't know how to act. What was right? Should he kiss her? Kneel down before her? Run away? Grab her? He tried remembering love scenes from movies he'd seen in the Bronx.

Suddenly Madame Lefebre rose, her hands briskly straightening her dress. She took a step away from the sofa, then stopped and turned to face Sylvan.

"You must go," she murmured. "Till your next lesson." She touched her fingers to her lips, then lightly placed her fingers on Sylvan's forehead.

"Go," she repeated.

Sylvan rose shakily, and stood before her.

"Yes," he said softly, thinking what should I do, what should I say, what do I want, what is right and what is wrong. . .

With a rush of courage, or stupidity, he blurted what he felt.

"I love you," Sylvan said.

"I love you, Sylvan. Go."

He went. That was the best lesson I've ever had, he thought as he floated along the sidewalk, hungrily looking forward to his next lesson.

Sylvan strolled the streets for hours; all that day, and all that night, and the next morning, Madame Lefebre was all he could think of. What would his next lesson bring? he wondered excitedly, feeling eagerness, fear, confusion, and, most of all, utter obsession.

He saw her face, and smelled her smell, and heard her voice, and felt her touch, everywhere. The strongest, and most peculiar, sensation was smelling her. It took Sylvan by surprise. It came to him at any odd moment, seemingly for no reason, sending a warm thrill of happiness all through him. He had no idea why the smell came when it came; it was not caused by smelling another, similar smell, nor by any other apparent external stimulus—it was pure memory.

An objective observer would not have called the smell pleasant. It was musky, dark, faintly acrid, but deep, rich, wet, and, of course, *her.* Sylvan thought of the soil under a long unmoved rock, and wet leaves, and sweat.

Never before had Sylvan *remembered* a smell. And the smell would bring with it an avalanche of sensations of memory that suffused him with her. He felt as though he was wading in a pool of her essence, drifting through the street or his room with mists of her eddying around his legs like affectionate cats or smoldering coals, or autumn leaves, or beach sand.

When Sylvan arrived at Madame Lefebre's door for his lesson the next day, she repeated her gesture of touching his brow with her kissed fingers, and they sat immediately at the piano.

Occasionally she would touch him lightly while he played, as though to signal tempo changes or a new key. And sometimes with a free hand he would touch her in return, tapping her knee or stroking her wrist.

Together they composed unrepeatable improvisations, the notes coming and going—beautiful and perfect—and finally disappearing, their presence inhaled, their passing not regretted as new clusters appeared in their place, only to be replaced. . .

And so the afternoons went, in love and music.

During the next few weeks, Sylvan's playing became more mellow, and he noticed a greater freedom in his improvisations. He wondered why.

"Love and composing are the same," Madame Lefebre said one afternoon. "Love is play; composing is play."

This made sense to Sylvan. When he played the piano, he thought about composing melodies on Madame Lefebre's lovely breasts. And when he was away from Madame, thinking about her, he imagined pounding octaves in the bass and startling chord progressions. Walking in the garden of her chateau, he saw love and compositions in the trees bending towards one another, in the architecture of the espaliered bushes growing side by side, in the afternoon clouds floating across the sky.

Months passed. He blossomed.

Meanwhile, back home in America, Sylvan's parents were disturbed. The first letters they received from their son had been filled with enthusiastic descriptions of Parisian life, cafe meetings with young intellectuals, visits to artists' quarters, growing fluency in the French language, and a fascination with Debussy and Ravel. These letters made his parents feel their money had been well spent; their son was benefiting from the artistic and intellectual milieu of Paris.

But then Sylvan's letters began to change. No longer did he write about picturesque Parisian streets; no longer did he pepper his letters with French phrases which sent his mother scurrying to her Larousse. Instead, his letters were filled with Madame Lefebre. It was obvious that Sylvan was in love.

"We didn't send him to Paris for this!" his mother exclaimed indignantly.

"At least he's having a good time," his father put in.

"We're not paying for that kind of good time, Harry. We sent him to Paris to learn about music, not about falling in love."

"Let the boy alone, Martha. Life is more than music, you know."

"You would say something stupid like that! Of course, life is more than music. Can't you say something constructive? What are we going to do about Sylvan?"

Harry looked exasperated. He started to say something, then changed his mind.

"You're *never* any help!" his wife hissed in frustration.

She stomped out of the room, entered the kitchen, and tried opening a can of sardines with her bare hands. Then she grabbed a chicken from the refrigerator and was about to cut it apart when someone knocked at the door.

"Who could that be?" she wondered, biting her tongue. She marched to the door and pulled it open. Sam was standing in the doorway, violin tucked under his arm.

"Why, Sam Ferdinand! Hello. Won't you come in."

"Thank you." Sam straightened his jacket and stepped inside. "I haven't seen you for awhile. How are you? And how is Sylvan?"

Mrs. Woods' jaw tightened. "I am terrible. Sylvan is worse.

"Really?"

"Terrible, terrible."

Sam looked alarmed. "What's wrong? Are you sick?"

"Yes, I'm sick—sick of worrying."

"Calm down, Mrs. Woods. Now tell me, what's the matter?"

"Sylvan is wasting away in Paris."

"Tuberculosis?"

"Worse."

"Cancer?"

"No, no."

"What is it, then?"

"He's in love."

There was a short pause. "Oh," Sam finally said with relief.

"Is that all you can say, Sam?"

"Love's not as bad as cancer," Sam offered, trying to save the situation. "What kind of girl is she?"

"She's not a girl."

"You mean—"

"That's exactly what I mean."

"I can't believe it. My best student is not *that* kind of boy."

"You better believe it; your best student *is* that kind of boy."

"I thought he'd have more taste."

"He doesn't."

"It's the way you raised him, Mrs. Woods," Sam said indignantly, "Always stuffing him with those chicken livers—"

"Don't criticize me, Sam Ferdinand! He would never have gotten in this mess if it hadn't been for you."

"Me?"

"Yes, *you.*"

Sam backed off. "Is the man handsome?" he asked.

"Man? What man?"

"Why, Sylvan's lover, of course."

"Sylvan's lover? What are you *talking* about, Sam? Sylvan's lover isn't a *man.*"

"No?"

"Of *course* not."

A silence slunk across the room. Sam's lips trembled. "You mean—it's a sheep?"

"What's the matter with you? You know Sylvan isn't *that* kind of boy."

"You just told me he was."

"I did not!"

"Well, let's not argue about a trivial point. I'm glad to hear he didn't get involved in . . . that kind of affair." Sam wandered over to the kitchen table and stared out the window. "Who is his lover?"

"His music teacher."

"Not Madame Lefebre!" he exclaimed.

Mrs. Woods nodded. "Madame Lefebre."

"Well, I'll be darned...."

"You can be darned, Sam, but I won't let this sort of thing continue."

Sam shook his head and smiled faintly. "She always had a unique way of teaching," he reminisced.

". . .What's that?"

"Oh, nothing."

"Listen, Sam. You know Madame Lefebre from the conservatory. You set up Sylvan's program with her. Is there anything you can do about this?"

Sam reflected a moment. "Have you written him?"

"Oh, yes, many times. But he's so in love, he doesn't even want to come home when the semester ends. He wants to stay in Paris another year and live with Madame Lefebre!" Mrs. Woods started to cry.

"Now, Mrs. Woods. It isn't that bad. It's just teenage infatuation. He'll get over it."

"Maybe he will—but *I* won't. Besides, we don't have enough money to keep him there another year. And I wouldn't pay for it anyway, even if I had it. The whole thing is preposterous."

"He won't come back of his own free will?"

"No."

"Sylvan is stubborn. Once he puts his mind to something, it's very hard to stop him." Sam put hands on hips and paced the kitchen floor. "Mrs. Woods, in order to bring Sylvan back, someone must go to Paris to get him."

"But we can't do that. We don't have the money or time—"

"Mrs. Woods," Sam put his hand on her shoulder. "I realize you can't go to Paris for your son. However, I can."

"You would really go to Paris?"

"Indeed."

Mrs. Woods was torn between hope and disbelief. "But, Sam, you're such a homebody. I thought you hated travel. You've often said the only thing that will make you leave home is money."

Sam stroked his chin. "Yes, I have said that. . . ." Then his eyes twinkled. "Now, Mrs. Woods, I want to tell you the *real* reason for my visit today. Of course, I always enjoy your cooking and the aroma of your kitchen. But, today I have wonderful news. I have been invited to Paris this summer to teach at the Fourneau Institut de Musique."

"Really, Sam? Why, that's wonderful. Is that a well-known school?" she asked. "I've never heard of it."

"Well-known? Why, the Fourneau Institut is one of the finest schools in the world for the training of young musicians. Many of its graduates are world-renowned—Gerald Toubov, or the pianist Pierre Machaud, for example. It is an honor to teach at the Institut."

Mrs. Woods was impressed. She knew Gerald Toubov's reputation as a virtuoso tuba player and as the first performer ever to give an entire concert on his knees. And Pierre Machaud—why, students flocked to the master classes in his swimming pool. She recalled meeting him briefly backstage after a concert on his most recent American tour and how politely he had shaken her hand, saying, "Zank you for the compliment, Mister."

"That's wonderful, Sam! You'll be in distinguished company." She broke into a happy smile. "And you'll be near Sylvan." Pointing to the kitchen table, she said, "Sit down for some fresh coffee and cake."

Sam removed his jacket, rolled up his sleeves, and sat at the head of the table. "Gladly," he said, "And would you add one of your delicious ham and lettuce sandwiches."

He continued talking through mouthfuls of food. "I knew Pierre Fourneau from the Conservatory, but I haven't seen him for years. Last week, I looked in my mailbox and what a surprise—a letter from good old Pierre. I opened it, and, *voila,* an invitation to teach at his Institut this summer! At first, I was a bit apprehensive. When I knew Pierre in Paris thirty years ago, he was a real crackpot. In fact, we nicknamed him 'Tete Cassee'—Broken Head. Once he invited me to his country home; when I got there, it didn't even exist. Another time, he insisted I sleep overnight at his apartment. 'Where's my bed?' I asked when I got there. He pointed to a painting of a bed hanging on the wall. 'Sleep in the picture' was his reply."

"If he's such a crackpot, why are you going?" Mrs. Woods asked, pouring coffee into his cup. "Won't it be unpleasant working for him?"

"I thought about that," Sam answered. "But there was a check in the envelope for half my salary, plus a one-way ticket to Paris. Maybe Pierre has changed."

"I hope so." Mrs. Woods poured herself some coffee. "Still, I can't understand why you would want to teach in Paris this summer. I know you always have an angle, Sam." She leaned over conspiratorially. "Is he paying you a lot of money?"

"Mrs. Woods, the pay is so low it is almost insignificant. I'm not going for the money. I'm going for the *prestige*. Do you *realize* what a credit teaching in Paris is? Students will flock to my door. I've dreamed about opening an *ecole de musique*. Paris will give me the credentials. Yes, there's money to be made in this business, and I plan to make it."

Mrs. Woods clasped her hands. "I'm so glad you're going. . . and you can tell Sylvan to come home."

"I'll tell him."

"Oh, Sam, you're an angel."

"I wish I were—I'd save on airfare." He took out a pen and wrote Fourneau's address on the back of his card. "I'll be leaving June 10th and staying in Montmartre. Don't worry. I'll visit Sylvan as soon as I get there."

The first thing Sam did in Paris was visit Pierre Fourneau. His old friend lived in a ten-room suite overlooking Avenue Foch. Fourneau had obviously come into money.

He had also gained a great deal of weight. When Sam rang the doorbell, he was greeted by a large round belly with a small Fourneau head sitting on top of it.

"*Bonjour*, Pierre!" Sam said, shaking Fourneau's hand. "*Mon Dieu*, you have grown."

"*Oui, c'est juste.*" Fournmeau patted his round belly. "Success has done this to me."

"I'm glad you're doing so well. Times have changed, eh? Not like conservatory days when you lived in that little rat-trap hole in Montmartre."

"Ah, *oui*," Fourneau reminisced. "How I detested that room. Two years ago, I bought the whole building. Now, for revenge, I rent it to my students."

"In spite of your pranks, Pierre, you always had a good head for business."

"*Oui*. That is why I am the success." Fourneau patted his belly again. "But, *mon ami*, you must be tired after your long voyage. We will discuss the details of your teaching schedule later." Fourneau scribbled something on a piece of paper and handed it to Sam. "First, get settled in your apartment."

Sam read the address. "Isn't this the same place—"

"All the rooms are redecorated," Fourneau assured. "They're very good."

Sam left his employer's suite to install himself in his new home. The narrow dark room, a block from the cemetery on Rue Lepic, faced the alley. Overflowing garbage cans stood in dreary contrast to the spacious opulence of Fourneau's quarters. "Such are the humble quarters of many artists," Sam sighed philosophically as he watched a family of cockroaches scatter across the rusty kitchen stove and disappear into a crack in the wall. Besides, he considered, brushing the elbows of his suit suspiciously, he would only be staying two months.

He put his suitcase on a chair and opened a closet next to the sink. A threadbare mop fell out. "The Lord of Music is telling me something," he groaned. Picking up the mop and choking its handle, he began mopping the floor furiously.

When he finished cleaning, he went to visit Sylvan.

Sylvan's apartment, on Rue St. Antoine near the Bastille, was not much better than Sam's. Instead of being on the first floor, it was a sixth-floor walk-up. As Sam trudged up the stairs, the halls got darker with each landing. By the fourth, he was panting and perspiring in Stygian darkness. The air was humid, and instead of becoming thinner—as usually happens—it was beginning to thicken. Foul odors emanated from beneath the closed apartment doors. When he reached the sixth-floor landing, the hall was so poorly lit that he could hardly make out the names on the doors. Then he noticed a narrow stairway heading still higher. Lowering his head to avoid the ceiling, he went up two more flights and finally arrived at a mouse-sized door. The nameplate read *Sylvan Woods.*

Sam knocked. The wood felt soft; a hinge creaked. He turned the knob and pushed. Gray light drifted into the hall-way.

"*Bonjour? Qui est-ce——*"

"Sylvan? Are you there?"

"Sam! Sam, what are *you* doing here?" Sylvan rushed over. "Great to see you!"

"It's great to see you, too, Sylvan," Sam replied, "only I can't see you. I can only hear you. Is there any light in this place?"

"All the lights are on."

"Oh."

"You get used to it."

"I suppose so. Must be good for learning Braille."

When Sam's eyes adjusted to the light, he took a longer look at Sylvan. The boy's hair was long and disheveled; he had grown a black mustache and a scraggly Vandyke, which elongated his thin face; above his faded jeans, strands of wool dangled from the edges of a pullover sweater.

Sam looked around the room. A cot stood next to a desk with two dilapidated chairs leaning against it. Books were piled in the corner.

"I've got so much to tell you, Sam. So many things have happened since my last letter."

"I'll bet."

"I know every street on the Left Bank. I can show you all the famous cafes, introduce you to my friends-"

"Yes, your friends. I'd like to talk to you about them."

"Good. They're great friends. How are things at home?"

"Politics as usual—prices going up, income going down. Politics as usual with your parents, too. Your father is still dreaming hazy dreams of freedom; your mother is shopping, cooking, and trying to run things. Nothing has changed with them. But they are concerned about you."

"Me? Why?"

"They think you've lost interest in your studies."

"That's not true. I'm working harder than ever. I just finished another composition the other day." Sylvan got down on his hands and knees and rummaged through a carton of papers stuffed under his bed. "Here it is. I should mail it to them to show how hard I'm working—but they can't read music, anyway."

Sam sat down on the bed. "Listen, Sylvan. I can level with you. What they're really worried about is you and Madame Lefebre."

"Why should they worry about us? We're doing fine."

"That's what they're worried about."

"But that should please them."

"It doesn't."

Sylvan started mashing the loose strands of his sweater between his fingertips. "I don't understand. When I love my music, they're happy; when I love a woman, they're not."

"That's the way they are." Sam reflected a moment. "But, you know, they have a point."

Sylvan looked betrayed.

"Wait a minute," Sam said. "I'm not against your love. I know Madame Lefebre is a wonderful woman and fine teacher, too. Still, your year here is ending. Your future is in America."

"What's my future without Madame Lefebre? I'd feel lost without her."

"Only temporarily lost. You have many new adventures ahead of you."

Sylvan thought Sam was wrong, but he listened. Sam always had an angle.

"There's nothing for me in the S t a t e s ...."

Sam lifted his finger in the air. "That's where you're wrong. There's *everything* for you in the States. Now you listen to me. Remember, I'm the one who suggested you spend a year in France. You were wise to follow my suggestion. Now, I *suggest you* return to America. It's time to go to college. And I believe the best college for you would be Westman School of Music."

Sylvan wrestled with conflicting possibilities. He thought about Madame Lefebre—her beautiful chateau, her beautiful mind and body, and the music they made together; he thought about the improvisations he had learned on her piano. Could it continue? The very fact that she was married, that he still called her Madame Lefebre instead of Jacqueline, and that she always referred to him as her "little puppy," suggested a certain inequality in their relationship.

He hated to admit it, but he knew Sam was right. "I've heard about Westman School," he said after a long silence. "Is it hard to get in?"

Sam chuckled. "The president and I used to play chamber music together. We're good friends. There'll be no problem getting in."

"Is it as good as they say it is?"

"Better. Not only do they give courses in every imaginable musical subject, but they believe in a practical philosophy which I also espouse; namely, that a musician should have a well-rounded education. Consequently, Westman has always insisted that their students study not only music, but languages, literature, history, physics, mathematics, mountain—climbing, even basketball."

Sylvan thought about Madame Lefebre again. "Sounds interesting," he said listlessly.

Sam moved closer. "Listen," he said, "I know you're disappointed about leaving France and especially about leaving Madame Lefebre. I don't blame you. Anyone would be. But life is full of chapters, and this one is closing. Close it gracefully, and you'll be able to begin the next one with new energy. Believe me, Westman School of Music is just the place for you."

Sylvan stared at the floor.

"Don't let me rush you, my boy. Think it over. All important decisions take time. You don't have to decide right away."

"What will I tell Madame Lefebre?"

"Don't worry about her. She's been through this before. Just tell her you have other obligations."

"That sounds cruel. Isn't there a better way I could phrase it?"

"My boy, sometimes life is cruel. But, remember, even when life seems bad—especially when it seems bad—it often means that something good is about to begin." He paused, then said gently, "Just tell her how you *feel* about leaving. Everything else will take care of itself."

A flushing toilet sounded through the pipes behind the walls. Sylvan pondered. Finally, he looked at Sam with a faint gleam in his eye. "You said they have basketball at Westman?"

Sam gave his protégé a fatherly pat on the knee. "Believe me, it's the right choice."

Sylvan stood up. His decision had been made. "Hey, I'm starving. Let's go downstairs for something to eat."

He closed the door to his apartment. As they went down the

stairs, the light at each landing grew brighter.

When Sylvan sat down at the piano for his lesson with Madame Lefebre, his playing was wild and feverish. He pounded the keys and stamped on the foot pedal.

Madame Lefebre knew something was wrong. "What is the matter?" she asked. "Are you suffering from bad dreams?"

"I'm fine," he answered, banging his elbow on top of the piano.

Madame Lefebre walked to Sylvan's side and whispered in his ear. "You are no longer composing, *petit chou*." Sylvan stopped playing and stared at the floor. "You're right," he sighed. "I can't concentrate."

"Why is that?"

"Bad dreams."

"I thought so." Madame Lefebre stroked Sylvan's cheek. "What are your bad dreams? Tell me about them."

"They're about you."

"Me? And they are bad dreams?" She pulled her hand away from Sylvan's face. "Bad dreams about me!"

Sylvan turned from the piano. "Really, they're bad dreams about me."

Madame Lefebre stroked his arm. "Come, come. Do I see a tear in your eye?"

"Probably. . . . Sam Ferdinand came to see me yesterday."

"Ah, Sam. He called me."

Sylvan spoke quickly. "We talked about my future. I'm going back to America to finish my education."

"Yes?"

"Yes." Sylvan covered his face with his hands. "I have to leave you! I'm sorry."

"What are you sorry about?"

"I don't want to leave you," he cried. "Life won't be the same without you."

"That is true. Still, you have *memoires*."

"I don't want *memoires*. I want you."

A distant look came into Madame Lefebre's eyes. "Life is pulling us in different directions. All we can have is *memoires*." She opened the drawer of her desk, took out a piano key, and handed it to Sylvan. "This will help you remember our lessons."

"I don't want an old piano key. I want you!"

"A piano key is all I can give."

Sylvan felt the key in his hand. It certainly felt different from Madame Lefebre. "Will you miss me?" he asked.

"Of course. I miss all of my little puppies. But little puppies grow up to become big dogs. Go into the world and become a big dog."

"I'll never forget you."

Madame Lefebre sat down on the couch. Leaning back, she spoke in a voice tinged with resignation. "That is my destiny—to be left but never forgotten."

"I'm sorry. Perhaps your husband could—"

"Do not speak of that thing!" she snapped. Then, softening her tone, "Sylvan, you are a talented musician. You are able to reach into your soul, draw out its love and hurt, and express it in your music. That is a great gift."

"I learned it all from you."

"No. I only helped you discover your voice."

He tried to kiss her, but she pushed him away. "No. None of that. Our lessons are over." She took a bottle of wine down from the shelf. Filling two glasses, she said, "Let us drink to your career."

Sylvan and Madame Lefebre finished three bottles of wine that afternoon. They did not sit at the piano for this their last lesson together. Rather, Madame Lefebre played for Sylvan record albums from her own past career as a soloist, and she related tales to him of the trials of being a solo artist: the fanatical commitment necessary to place *everything* second to your art. Sylvan felt in awe of such dedication, and told himself that he was indeed such a person. By the time Sylvan left Madame Lefebre's chateau, he had almost forgotten her. But he held the piano key tightly as he staggered up the stairs to his apartment.

CHAPTER SIX

Linda

WHEN SYLVAN ARRIVED AT Westman School of Music, he was given a dormitory room on the second floor of Mozart Hall. Looking out of his window, he had an excellent view of the fraternity quadrangle where pledges were running in circles, tossing Frisbees to one another.

Westman School was located in the town of Rochester in upstate New York. Its forty rolling acres faced the Lethe River and a cement plant. Pastures with grazing cows, enclosed by barbed wire fences, surrounded the school. Whenever these fences were broken, cows wandered into the campus, often peering through the first-floor windows and listening to lectures on Baroque counterpoint. Many brass players milked the cows, bottled the milk, and sold it in the student cafeteria.

Cows had always played an important role in the history of Westman School. Their mooing had been a theme in many symphonies of young composers; their manure, often left on sidewalks, lawns, and doorways, was used to fertilize fraternity gardens. Beta Phi—the bassoon fraternity—sold vegetables from its garden to professors in return for higher marks. Although the Westman catalog never mentioned the effect of cows on student morale, their soft eyes and vast expanse of hide formed an important part of campus life. The gentle mooing of a Guernsey reminded students of peace beyond scholarship; the swishing tails symbolized the ease with which an accomplished musician could whisk away theory problems or self-doubts.

Sylvan joined a group of freshmen on a tour of the campus. "Westman School of Music is an extraordinary school," their senior guide proclaimed in a rich baritone voice, specially trained for orientation week. "Our founder, the market speculator, Hedy Westman, had Mozart Hall and the Beethoven Barracks built in the spring of 1929. In the fall of that year, he committed suicide. The board of directors wanted to close the school, but the students *refused* to give up their education! They started a protest bonfire which spread over 450 acres of hayfield and received national attention. A dairy company, Galaxy Farms, came to the rescue. They promised to finance the college for one year if the students would work without pay cutting hay, milking cows, and driving milk trucks. The students accepted."

The audience of freshmen listened in rapt attetion.

"All your music courses will take place here," the senior continued as they passed the Gothic buildings on Music Row. "Behind these stone structures are wooden ones where you will study science and the humanities—disciplines representing a plus in Westman. A union of all disciplines is our goal. Hopefully, you will learn to express this union through your music."

On his second day of classes, Sylvan got his first term paper assignment from his History of Music professor. To research it, he went to the college library. He found Beethoven in the "B" section of the card catalog, then headed down the stairs to the stacks. He passed rows of eight-foot bookshelves filled with thousands of books. Dazzling! He was standing in a treasure chest. So many secrets lay before him, so many voyages and ideas. Where would he begin?

He came upon an alcove. Tucked away in a corner were carrels where students could read and meditate in solitude. Here, far from the illusions, noises, and odors of the outside world, he experienced a beautiful feeling of inner peace.

Then he noticed a leg sticking out of a carrel. Its foot was covered by a Chinese slipper and cotton sock. Above the sock hung the bottom of loose dungarees.

Sylvan wondered if there was more to this leg.

He tip-toed over and peeked behind the metal screen. Long black hair flowed over a cotton blouse; white arms spread across the desk; an assured hand was busy writing. Sylvan inhaled the aroma of freshly washed hair.

Boldly, he broke the silence. "What are you writing?"

The girl's brown eyes squinted as she looked up from her paper; she faced Sylvan with a distant expression.

"Sorry, I didn't mean to disturb you."

She blinked, then turned back to the desk and resumed writing.

She was beautiful! He stood transfixed. How could he get her to talk to him? He knew she wanted to be left alone. Yet, if he didn't meet her now, there might not be another chance.

While deciding what to do, he pulled a book off the shelf. He glanced through it as he sneaked glimpses of her. He pulled other books off the shelf. Soon, piles of unopened volumes lay scattered around him. A seventeen-hundred-page reference book slipped out of his hands and crashed to the floor.

The girl looked up, annoyed. "Please be quiet!"

"Sorry. I'm just overwhelmed by all these books."

"Maybe it's your hands," she hissed through her perfect teeth.

"Nothing wrong with my hands. I'm a violinist."

"So?"

"I just mean my hands are okay. They've been trained. Dropping the book was an accident. I'm sorry."

"Well. . . . Apology accepted."

Sylvan glanced at her feet. "Why are you wearing Chinese slippers?"

"They're better for dancing," she answered, slowly draping her leg over the chair in front of her. What a leg! Muscular, curvaceous. The right side had been shaved; the left side had stubs of hair. "I designed them to fit the mode of medieval women," she explained, turning her leg to give Sylvan a better view of her shapely gastrocnemius. "Shaving symbolizes the purity of Jesus—the uncorrupted Roman church of Pope Gregory; the unshaved side reminds me of heretics, namely the Albigensians. They're my favorites."

"Mine, too."

"You know the Albigensians?"

"Who doesn't?" Sylvan had made an impression. Luckily, he had read about the 12th-century Albigensian heresy in southern France in *Medieval Gregorian Chants and Their Children* by Holder and Bache. Also, Madame Lefebre had mentioned them during one of her lessons.

"They were terrific," said the girl. "Their heresies inspire me to study for this stupid accounting test."

"Accounting?"

"You've got to take accounting before you graduate Westman. I figured I'd take it my freshman year and get it over with."

"That's smart. I'm a freshman, too."

"You are? I'd never guess it from your height."

"What does height have to do with it?"

"I don't know. I just thought all freshmen were short."

"That's narrow-minded of you—"

"Listen, dope." The words shot out like bullets. Her sudden anger surprised Sylvan. "My mind's in good shape. I've been shrunk by the best. At least I know why I'm here. Do you?"

"You mean why I'm at Westman?"

"Yes." She twirled her pencil around all five fingers, a trick Sylvan had only seen magicians perform. "Why did you come to Westman? To bother me?"

"Look, don't get defensive."

"Who's defensive?"

"You are. . .uh . . ." Sylvan fumbled. "What's your name?"

"Linda Kouras."

"I'm Sylvan Woods."

Silence.

"Don't get defensive," Sylvan repeated. "In answer to your question: I came to Westman to get a well-rounded education."

"Oh?" She paused. "Where did you read that?"

"You're so sarcastic. Why did you come here?"

"I'm in medieval studies."

Sylvan remembered his trips to the Metropolitan Museum—knights in armor, woven tapestries, wooden cabinets carved with religious figures—a bleak, mysterious, other-worldly existence.

"Do you study Latin?" he asked. "And the Renaissance?"

"No, only alchemy."

"What's that?"

"Alchemists tried turning base metals into gold."

"That's impossible. . . . Did they succeed?"

"I don't know. But I'm going to." She stroked her chin while reflecting on her determination. "Of course, I'm not working with metals. I'm working with myself."

"What do you mean?"

"I'm changing my personality—from base metal into gold. It's something you ought to think about."

"That's silly. You can't change personalities."

"That's what *you* say. But what do you know? Have you ever been in therapy?"

"No."

"Well, there's your answer."

"Therapy's not everything."

"No, there's also Bar Mitzvah."

Sylvan shook his head. "You're weird. Your mind jumps like a jelly bean. Therapy, Bar Mitzvah. What do they have to do with each other?"

"My mind jumps because I'm a Gemini." She rose from her seat. "I need to stretch." She faced Sylvan and started doing *plies* in front of him. Holding the edge of her desk like a bar, she *plied* in all five ballet positions, did leg extensions, *grand battements, jetes, ronds de jambes*, turns, *pointe* work, and *pas de bas*, before ending the routine in a stately arabesque with right hand extended almost to Sylvan's nose. He held her hand while she balanced easily on her right toes.

"You move beautifully," he said with admiration. "I love those—"

"Shut up! Can't you see I'm concentrating?"

"Sorry."

Linda concentrated on her arabesque. Then she relaxed, dropped Sylvan's hand, and sat down in her chair.

"I've always admired dancers," Sylvan said. "I'd love dancing, but I'm a klutz. I'm good in music, but somehow, I just can't translate it into my feet."

"You could be graceful with a little effort. You may be a klutz, but it's more in the head than in your feet. It's a matter of attitude."

"Yeah, maybe. I play basketball; but as for dancing, well—I can't do it. I can't even social dance. I'm too inhibited."

"I used to be inhibited, too," Linda explained. "But no more. I've been cured of that."

"Really? That's good." Sylvan pondered a moment. "But aren't inhibitions tough to get rid of? How do you do it?"

"I keep a journal. I write in it every day, anything that comes to mind. I'm amazed at what comes to mind, sometimes. But I write it down no matter what. And by writing it, I free myself. I see what I've been thinking about; it's right there, down on paper. The more I write, the less inhibited I become. By writing, I found out I was an unusual person. I liked colors, exotic clothing, things I never would have imagined before. . . ."

"Did you ever want to become a writer?" Sylvan asked.

Linda surveyed the hundreds of books shelved around her; she sniffed the air as if to smell the aging books, their distant thoughts, philosophies of bygone ages.

"Good question," she mused, "but impossible to answer. I've wanted to become so many things, I've lost track. When I was a kid on Long Island, I spent weekends in the Metropolitan Museum roaming from one century to another. I bought a notebook; I copied paintings and sculptures by the masters. They inspired me. I thought of becoming an artist; but after copying medieval triptychs and those crazy paintings by Hieronymus Bosch, I decided to become a medievalist, instead. Before that, I considered ballet, guitar, piano, languages, philosophy, medicine, history. You name it, I thought about it. Right now, it's medieval studies. But who knows? Tomorrow, maybe something else. I've got a voracious appetite for new things. I want to explore everything."

"But medieval studies," Sylvan was puzzled. "That's not new. It's pretty dusty and old."

"Now you're the one who's narrow-minded. The old can be new; the new can be old. It's a matter of perspective. Most people have forgotten what life in the Middle Ages was like. It's so old and forgotten, it's new."

"You're fun to talk to."

"You, too."

Sylvan glanced at his watch. "Wow, we've been here an hour! I'm late for Music Theory. Can we meet again? How about lunch?"

"Can't do it until Wednesday."

"That's okay. I'll meet you here at one. We'll go to Clancy's."

"Good. I like that place."

CHAPTER SEVEN

Drained Out

CLANCY'S WAS NOT ONLY a student hangout. It was a historic bar, too. Entrants were soon made aware of this fact. The hallowed head of Hedy Westman stood in strategic positions all around the bar. It hung on oil paintings beneath the eaves. A stone-carved bust stood on a pillar next to the juke box, whose selections included only music written by former Westman composers plus one recording of Beethoven's Pastoral, composed, said the caption, in memory of cows he had known. Books by Lawrence Tidbit, composer of the school anthem, *Westman, You Give Yeast For My Yearning*, stood on the top shelf of the Bar Bibliotheque. (Clancy's had its own lending library. However, books from this library couldn't be lent very far since each one was tied to the stacks by a seven-foot chain. Borrowers sat at the adjoining table.)

Clancy's became a second home for Sylvan and Linda. Month after month, year after year, they repaired to the friendly beer resort, sitting at their favorite table in the corner next to the fireplace and beneath the stuffed cowhead on the wall. There, in the semidarkness of thirty-watt bulbs, they sat facing each other in the sturdy old wooden "Clancy chairs" that dated back to the founding of the school.

One winter day they sloshed in wearing galoshes and dragging scarves and heavy winter coats across the floor.

"They just finished plowing Dapner Street," Sylvan said, pulling off his fur-lined coat and draping it around the back of his chair. He sat down and unbuckled the tops of his galoshes. "This is the worst storm we've had in three years."

Linda hung her knee-length coat on a wall hook, and pulled off her sweater. "A fitting climax to exam week."

"How'd you do?"

"Latin was a breeze, and so was Archeology." She called the waiter for two beers. "Eighteenth-century Counterpoint was tough. Blinderbode always gives tricky exams. He asked us to write out all fugal parts to Bach's *St. Matthew Passion*. I broke my head on that question. Who can remember those things? I just made up a fugue and let it go at that. Afterwards, I found out there *were* no fugues and that my answer should have been a blank. What a pill that guy is! A real sadist!"

"I know," Sylvan agreed, taking off his galoshes and pushing them under his chair. "I had him for two weeks last year before I switched out. All he could talk about was how Bach's sex life influenced his bass note progressions. The guy is sick."

"Exams are so stupid. They should abolish them."

"Yeah."

The waiter put two beers on their table. Linda relaxed, leaned back in her chair, and guzzled half the glass. "How'd you make out, Sylvan?"

"Okay, I guess. Either tests are getting easier, or I'm getting smarter. Philosophy was a cinch. I got Spinoza down cold—did a great essay on him. I got all the conjugations in German. Electronic Music was multiple choice, or multiple chance, whatever you want to call it. I'm sure I'll pull an 'A' in that one."

"How about Orchestration?"

"We had to arrange twenty-four measures of Stravinsky's *Rite of Spring* for oboe, bass, and viola. What a stupid combo! It wasn't hard, though."

"Seems like you did all right." Linda sipped her beer. "Did Giocinni give you a violin test?"

Sylvan mirthless grin belied his victory. "He's the toughest tester of them all. But I did well on that one, too."

"What's his test like?"

"You know Giocinni—a real intellectual. For the last three years, he's been emphasizing this intellectual approach to the violin. He's written two books on it."

"Different from Sam."

"Opposite as night and day."

"I never liked Giocinni," Linda said. "He's a cold fish."

"How do you know? You've never had him."

"I pass him in the halls. I look into his eyes, and they're dead. Dead iris, dead cornea, dead everything. They're only alive when he blinks."

"He is kind of laid back—"

"Laid back! You mean laid out! The guy's a creep, a walking corpse. I don't know why he's teaching music. He'd be better off in a mortuary school, teaching flower-arranging for funerals."

"Take it easy, Linda. Don't attack someone you don't know. I've learned a lot from Giocinni. I'm indebted to him for what he's given me."

"Ha, that's a laugh. What's he given you?"

"He's taught me how to *think* when I play the violin."

"Oh? How does he do that?"

"He taught me to concentrate on each note before playing it. I've tightened up my playing because of him. I've stopped improvising. Giocinni thinks improvising is wrong, an insult to the composer. When we began lessons, he vowed to straighten out my playing and my performing. The way I performed Mendelssohn in high school was terrible—an insult to the composer."

Linda shook her head. "There's something sinister about the way he walks," she muttered. "Tell me more about these funeral arrangements."

"Funeral arrangements?"

"Yes. Giocinni's going to kill your playing. And you're helping him."

"What are you talking about? Giocinni's helped me. I agree with him. After all, why should a composer write music if he doesn't expect a performer to play it as written?"

Linda shook her head again. "What you're saying sounds good," she said sadly. "It even sounds right. The problem is, it's *wrong*. Giocinni is a letter-of-the-law man; he mechanically follows every note and word that's been written. But, by paying such close attention to what's been written, he loses the spirit of the music. In fact, any true feeling expressed through music would probably frighten him."

"How can you say that?" Sylvan protested. "You don't even know him."

"I told you, I know by the way he walks." She looked directly at Sylvan. "I can also tell by the way your violin playing has deteriorated."

"What!"

"You know what I mean."

"I do not! Explain yourself."

"Sylvan, face it. Over the last three years, your playing has lost its zip. There's no magic left in it—and hardly any emotion. You used to play with such zest. I remember the first time I heard you."

"You mean in the Briggs Hall basement?"

Linda brightened. "What a great night!"

"But most of the audience walked out on me."

"True, but those who stayed witnessed a memorable event."

Sylvan waved her away with his hand. "Bah, that's kid stuff. It's okay for freshmen. But I'm a senior. Giocinni taught me not to fool around anymore. I'm more serious now."

"I've noticed."

"What's wrong with being serious?"

"Nothing. Serious is fine." She sipped her beer, then pushed her glass to the center of the table. "Remember the charge," she went on, "when our class captured the sophomore flag? You weren't in the charge. No, not you. You stood under a tree and threw chunks of manure at the sophomores. It distracted them, and we won. Peculiar. Novel." She laughed, remembering it. "I liked that. And the tug-of-war? We were up to our knees in mud when you greased their rope. Quick thinking. I liked that, too. Improvising on the Mendelssohn and Tartini's *Devil's Trill,* the way you played them. Wow! It inspired me." Linda grabbed Sylvan's arm; she shook his sleeve. "Remember your Mozart paper? You cleaned out the library for that one, dragged hundreds of books to your room, piled them on your desk, on the chair, on the bed, under the bed, everywhere. What enthusiasm! I loved you for it." She pointed to the ceiling. "You had *personal visits* from Him. I envied you. Dancing, whistling through the halls, singing in the lunchroom. . . ." She sat back and sighed. "Soon you'll be graduating, Sylvan. Where's the magic now? Where's it gone?"

"Well, uh— "

"Dr. Giocinni ruined you!"

Sylvan tried again. "He's not that bad."

"Sylvan, stop fooling yourself. There's been a change in you.

He hesitated. "Yes, I've changed—and it's for the better. I'm more intellectual now."

Linda was silent. He waited. Her silence continued.

"Well," he stumbled, "maybe it's true. Something *is* missing. I don't know if it's college, my age, or what; but something has drained out of me." He reflected a long moment. "Once I felt in touch with a secret power. What attacks I had then! But I haven't had an attack for months. I'm losing it." He looked sadly down at the floor. "There are other things on my mind, too."

Linda listened.

"What will I do after graduation?" Sylvan asked. "What will *we* do? I lie awake thinking about those questions."

"I guess we'll always see each other," Linda offered.

"You're pretty casual about it. Let's plan something more definite."

"Like what?"

"Like getting married."

"Are you joking?"

"Other people do it."

"Other people aren't us, Sylvan."

"What's wrong with getting married?"

"Nothing's wrong with it. But first you need a job, a direction—you have to know what you want."

"I thought you just have to be in love."

"Love helps, but it's not everything."

Sylvan leaned forward. "Let's try it anyway."

"Sylvan, I'm not ready to get married, and neither are you. What are you going to do? You've given up the idea of performing or teaching."

"That's true," Sylvan agreed, "but I'll find something else." He took another sip of beer. "What about you?"

"My father wants me to work in his restaurant."

"In other words, after we graduate, we'll just be friends."

"It looks that way."

Sylvan slumped in his chair. Linda touched his hand gently. "Don't look so gloomy," she said. "Being friends isn't so bad. Besides, who can tell what the future will bring?"

"I can tell," Sylvan muttered, slowly tearing up his placemat and tossing the pieces into the ashtray.

"Sylvan, it's not the end of the world. It's not the end of *you*. Why be defeated? Where's your self-esteem?"

"Self-esteem? *You're* my self-esteem!"

"I'm not your self-esteem. You can't find it outside of you. When we separate, it'll hurt us both, but it won't affect our self-esteem."

"It'll affect mine. Mine's going to zero."

"Oh, stop whining."

"I'm losing you!"

Sylvan sulked in silence. He bit his beer glass as he took another drink. It tasted more bitter than usual. "You pay the bill!" he finally snapped.

"Me?"

"Yes, you."

"I didn't bring money."

"I don't care."

"You're the one who brings the money."

"Maybe. But tonight you pay. It's time you did something for yourself."

"Stop being spiteful, Sylvan."

"Paying is good for you. It'll prepare you for the outside world. It'll make you a better person."

"You're bulldozing me."

"Linda, I can't keep paying for you. I don't have a job. We won't be together much longer, anyway. We might as well start practicing independence now."

Her face turned red. "Cut out this power game. You and your money can't bulldoze me!" She slammed the table with her fist. "You're always squawking about being independent. Pay the bill!"

Sylvan rose from the table. "I will not! Starting tonight, we're on our own—you and me both." He grabbed his coat and headed for the exit. "*Independence!*" he shouted across the table. "We'll start practicing it *now!*"

He slammed Clancy's exit door shut. An icy gust cut across his face as he stamped down the snow-plowed street. He hardly felt the cold. Independent and alone, he headed with a determined step towards the darkened campus.

Lost

CHAPTER EIGHT

A Family Tradition

WHEN SYLVAN CAME HOME from Westman, he went to visit Sam Ferdinand. The walls of his teacher's apartment on 181st Street were lined with books. Rays of afternoon sunlight illuminated the manuscripts lying on top of the piano. Sam sat on the arm of a sofa.

"So, you're bored," he said.

Sylvan nodded. "Yes."

"Your career in music has come to an end?"

"I think so."

Sam stroked his chin thoughtfully. "An old road ends; a new road begins."

"What is that supposed to mean?"

"It means it's time for a change. Time to try something different, something you've never done before."

"Like what?"

Sam rose. He paced the room with eyes fixed on the carpet as he wrestled with the problem. Suddenly, he snapped his fingers. "I've got it! I know just the job for you."

"What is it?"

"Sylvan, you have music in your blood," Sam explained, "but for some reason, you cannot recognize this now. Who knows when you will recognize it. I can't predict the future—I have enough trouble with the present. Someday you will find your place in music. In the meantime, though, while you are searching, you still have to make a living. . . ."

"Don't give me a lecture, Sam. Give me a direction."

Sam paused, raised his right hand, and pointed to the south. "I am giving you a direction, the direction of Wall Street. I am sending you to Herman Schlossberger to become a stockbroker."

"What!"

"A stockbroker. It's just the job for you."

"But I don't even know what a stockbroker is. What's a stockbroker?"

"A stockbroker is someone who sells stocks."

"But I don't know anything about stocks."

Sam scratched his chin. "All the more reason to become a stockbroker."

"But, Sam, who'll hire me if I don't know anything?"

"Herman Schlossberger will hire you. Aah, Sylvan, you have a lot to learn. In many brokerages, knowing nothing is a prerequisite for landing a job. Many of these firms want people whose minds are totally empty to begin with. They put you through a training program and fill you with all kinds of necessary and unnecessary information about stocks, bonds, price earnings ratios, and what have you."

"Well, I don't know," Sylvan stammered.

"You may not know, but I do! Sylvan, becoming a broker is just right for you at this time. You need something completely different—and this is it."

"But I don't even know how to find such a job."

"Finding a job is no problem. My old student—Herman Schlossberger—is a broker with Schleswig, Holstein, Berlin, and Zolongue. Herman was a terrible violinist, but was always very good at trading. In fact, when he was twelve years old, he traded in his violin lessons for a bicycle." Sam punctuated the air with an exclamation point. "But the most fascinating thing about Herman is his uncanny ability to predict the future."

"Really?" Sylvan's eyes lit up. "You mean he can actually predict it?"

"I remember his first prediction," Sam continued. "He predicted the stock market would fall 100 points. Sure enough, he was right. Over a three-year period, it fell 100 points."

"That's fantastic! Predicting the future. I don't know anyone who can do that."

Sam had touched Sylvan's imagination. From now on, the problems would only be technical. "I think you should meet Herman," he said. "You two have a lot in common."

"I'd like that. Maybe he could even predict my future."

Sam had a satisfied look on his face. "Maybe," he hummed, "maybe."

Sylvan was full of enthusiasm when he returned home; he couldn't wait to begin his new life. Bursting into the living room, he found his father snoring on the couch and his mother sitting in her armchair reading a mystery thriller. "Pa, wake up," he cried. "Ma, listen to this! I'm getting a job as a stockbroker!"

His father grunted, rolled over on his back, and kept snoring. His mother looked up from her book. "Be quiet," she whispered. "Can't you see your father is sleeping?"

"Ma, I'm too excited."

"Ssh, ssh, what are you excited about?" she implored, slowly closing her book.

"Listen. One of Sam's old students is now a stockbroker on Wall Street. I'm going to call him up for a job." His mother wrinkled her brow in bewilderment. "Sam arranged the whole thing," Sylvan added.

"You, a stockbroker? What do you know about stocks?"

"Nothing. But I can learn. They have a training program."

On hearing the word "stockbroker," Harry Woods sighed, grunted again, and opened one eye.

"Stocks?" his mother asked, shaking her head. "Sylvan, you must be mad."

"No, Ma, I need a change. Stocks may be the answer."

The word "stocks" caused Harry Woods to open both eyes and sit up.

"Sylvan, we did not send you to college to become a stockbroker," his mother continued disapprovingly, "but to study, to learn, to become a fine violinist, and perhaps even a world-renowned musician—but now, *this*. A stockbroker?" Her lips curled downwards in a sneer. "What is the meaning of this idea?"

"But, Ma, it's a well-respected profession. Besides, I need a rest from music."

"Not *that* kind of rest."

"The lad is right," Harry Woods broke in, moving to the edge of the couch. "Too much music can confuse the brain. Stocks could very well be the answer."

"You shut up!" his wife snapped. "It's none of your business."

"What do you mean, none of my business?"

Martha Woods turned down her volume. "Harry, don't act like such a baby. Stop whining and go back to sleep."

"Martha, the boy needs guidance."

"And who's going to give it to him? You? Ha, that would be

a laugh!"

"Martha, I insist—"

"Harry, if you don't shut up right now, I'm going to let out *your secret.*"

"My secret?"

"Yes, I'm warning you! Stay out of this, or everyone, including your son, will know."

"You wouldn't."

"I would."

Torn between anger and fear, Harry retreated. Then, a look of determination crossed his face. "A stockbroker's job would be good for Sylvan."

Martha Woods turned red. "That would be the worst thing for Sylvan! You would say something stupid like that, you. . .you gambler! There, I said it, you *gambler!*"

Harry winced. His wife pointed at him. "Gambler! Gambler! Gambler!" she shouted, shaking her finger. "You and your crummy stocks! We'd be rich if you hadn't lost so much on stocks! Gambler! Gambler!" she shouted again, tears of frustration in her eyes.

"Now, dear, it's nothing to cry about—"

Sylvan was fascinated. "Dad, you mean, you buy stocks?"

"I've bought a few in my day."

"A few!" Sylvan's mother cried. "A few! You call twenty stocks a few? And that's just for this month. What will happen next month or the month after?" She wiped her eyes with the edge of her apron. "What's worse is, they only go down."

"I've had a few paper losses—"

"A few! That's your favorite word—few." Mrs. Woods paced the floor. "When are you going to face your disease?"

"Wow, Dad, I didn't know you played the stock market."

"Sometimes I do."

"Sometimes," his mother hissed. "All times!"

"Then," Sylvan said, "if I took a job as a stockbroker, I'd be following a family tradition."

"That's true in a sense," his father agreed.

"Oh, God. . . ." Mrs. Woods groaned.

"It's always good to do something in a family tradition," Sylvan proclaimed.

"No! Sylvan, if you do this, I-I-I don't know what I'll do."

"But, Ma, it's a family tradition."

"It's a family disgrace. Stay away from it!"

"Martha, calm down. The boy is old enough to make his own decisions."

Sylvan's mother turned on her heels and stamped out of the room.

"Thanks for the advice, Dad."

Sylvan's father smiled to himself and leaned back on the couch.

CHAPTER NINE

Wall Street

S YLVAN TELEPHONED HERMAN SCHLOSSBERGER to set up an appointment for the following week. Then he spent three days reading everything he could find in the library on the subject of money.

On Monday morning, after a long subway ride, he stood before a forty-story building overlooking Wall Street and the East River. Squeezing into the elevator, he felt his stomach sink as it shot up to the thirty-fifth floor. When he stepped out, his feet sank into a plush rug. Adjusting his tie, straightening his jacket, and burping nervously, he pulled open the door across which the name *Schleswig Holstein Berlin Zolongue* was painted in gold letters.

"I have an appointment with Herman Schlossberger," he told the secretary behind the desk.

She pointed down the hall. "That way." Sylvan walked past a drinking fountain and bathroom before entering a large room filled with desks. Behind each desk, brokers in shirt sleeves were answering phones, shuffling papers, or making purchase entries in their account books. To the left was a row of paneled doors. On the first, the name *Herman P. Schlossberger* was written in Gothic script.

"This must be it," Sylvan thought. He knocked on the door.

"Come in."

Sylvan pushed the door open. A white-haired man was sitting behind his desk, shuffling papers.

"Mr. Schlossberger?"

The man kept shuffling.

"Herman Schlossberger?"

"Oh, Hermes," he gestured towards the wall with a hitch-hiker's thumb. "Next room."

Sylvan knocked on the next door.

"Come in!" roared a bass voice. Sylvan entered an office cluttered with newspapers, magazines, and reports. Behind a wide desk covered with telephones and scratch pads sat a heavy, jowl-faced man in his mid-forties.

Sylvan stepped into the room. "Hello, Mr. Schlossberger. I'm Sylvan Woods."

Mr. Schlossberger took the cigarette out of his mouth. "Who?" he asked.

"Sylvan Woods. Remember, I called you last week about a job?"

Just then, the phone rang. Schlossberger grabbed it like a hungry lion clawing a piece of meat.

"Yeah," he chewed.

Just then, another phone rang. Schlossberger took it with his other hand.

"Yeah." Then, with a phone at each ear, Schlossberger began carrying on two conversations at once. Out of the right side of his mouth, he told a customer to sell Gulf and Western; from the left side of his mouth came the words: "Buying options on Westing-house."

The calls ended. Schlossberger took out his pen and jotted

down a few notes. He didn't bother using paper but simply wrote them directly on his desk. He looked up at Sylvan.

"I'm Sylvan Woods. Remember? I called you last week—"

"How'd you get into my office!" roared Schlossberger.

"Wha—

"Get outta here, you little turd! How dare you come into my office!" Schlossberger banged his fist so hard on the desk that one of the phones jingled. He grabbed the receiver, but quickly hung up when no one answered.

"But I have an appointment with you," Sylvan pleaded, completely startled by this turn of events.

Schlossberger hesitated a moment. He put on his thick black-rimmed glasses. "Huh," he grunted.

"I have an appointment. Remember? I'm the one Sam Ferdinand recommended?"

"Huh." Schlossberger looked Sylvan over again, reappraising the situation. "For a moment there, I thought you were my son."

"Oh, no, sir, I'm not your son at all. Sylvan Woods is my name. Remember? Sylvan Woods? The one Sam Ferdinand recommended?"

"What kinda crap is this? I don't remember a call from you. And who is this Sam Ferdinand creep? Part of the mob, too?"

"Sam Ferdinand. He was your old violin teacher."

"Violin?"

"Yes. Don't you remember? You took violin lessons with him long ago."

Schlossberger's hulking body rocked from side-to-side while his jaw moved spasmodically. "Oh, yeah. You mean Sammy. I remember Sammy. A good guy."

"Yes, Sammy. That's it," Sylvan put in eagerly. "Sam Ferdinand. A good guy."

"Yeah. He was my fiddle teacher. A good guy. . . ."

The phones started ringing again. For the next two hours, Schlossberger was all over his desk, writing messages, shouting orders, slamming down phones, and generally acting like an outpatient on the verge of an epileptic fit. At 12:15 p.m., the phones stopped ringing.

"Let's go to lunch, kid," he said. "Can't talk here."

Twenty minutes later, Sylvan was seated opposite Schlossberger on the ground floor of the posh Stockhouse Restaurant. Their window overlooked a traffic jam on Broadway. Sylvan felt uncomfortable. He was not used to such elegant dining. Sinking into the cushion of his chair, he surveyed the restaurant. Waiters in tuxedos scurried noiselessly across the carpeted floor carrying drinks, trays of dishes, and half grapefruits; reproductions of 17th-century Flemish masters hung on the walls; the lights were dim; in the center of the room was a stone basin surrounded by statues of naked nymphs shooting water into the air through their noses and smiling beatifically at the ceiling.

"Eat, kid," Schlossberger commanded paternally. "It's on me.

Sylvan picked up the menu and flipped it open to page 13. His eyes fell on the cheapest item, a slice of rye bread priced at $5.95. He leafed through the rest of the menu, which was laid out like an Annual Report. The first few pages gave a concise history of the Stockhouse Restaurant. Colorful photographs of patrons slopping soup and wiping their mouths with linen napkins accompanied the history, which was written in both French and English.

The menu was presented in the following manner:

Assets

    Turkey, $17.95—sans *plume (without feathers), 8.95*
    French legumes, $11.50

Steak with mushrooms, $21.50

Liabilities

Waiters, $130.00 per week

Dishwashers, $98.50 per week

Chef, $475.00 per week

Stockholder's Equity

One Farm in Allendale, PA, $70,000 *(see Footnote II)*

Sylvan turned to the footnote. It read: 46 cows *valued at $948.95, depreciated at 5% per year using straight-line method; manure assessed at full market value; farm fixtures and building depreciated, amortized, condemned, and forgotten.*

"I've never seen a menu like this before," said Sylvan.

"Just order a hamburger," grumbled Schlossberger, pointing to the Steak and Mushrooms. "We got a lot to talk about."

While waiting for their order, Sylvan questioned the broker about his past. "How did you like your lessons with Sam?" he asked.

"Lessons?"

"Violin lessons."

A vacant look crossed Schlossberger's face. "Violin?"

"Yes, violin lessons with Sam Ferdinand—remember?"

"Oh, yeah, Sammy ... That was a long time ago."

"Do you still play?"

"Play what?"

"The violin."

Suddenly, Schlossberger broke out in the strangest soprano laugh—a cross between a giggle and a shriek. The customers seated nearby turned to stare. Startled waiters and the maitre d' rushed towards the table, fearing an attack of indigestion and a subsequent law suit. Then, just as suddenly as he had started,

Schlossberger stopped. His face turned stone sober. "Don't ever ask me about the violin again!" he growled. "It makes me sad."

"I'm sorry. I won't do it again."

Schlossberger fixed his eyes on Sylvan, then relaxed. His gaze wandered around the restaurant; the preoccupied look returned.

Sylvan tried again. "How did you get interested in the stock market?"

"Who?"

"You."

"I've always been in the market."

Sylvan fished for another question to break the tense silence. "How . . . er . . . does the stock market work?"

"Works fine." Schlossberger ordered a shot of straight gin and dumped it in his clam chowder.

Another long pause. "Mr. Schlossberger, you said you had a lot to talk to me about."

"Yeah."

"Can I hear some of it?"

"Yeah."

"What is it?"

"You're gonna be my assistant."

Sylvan's face lit up. "Really?"

Schlossberger toasted their new relationship by clinking his soup bowl with Sylvan's water glass.

"I appreciate this. It's awfully kind of you. But, I hope you realize, I know nothing about the stock market. I hardly even know what a stock is."

Schlossberger blinked.

"And you still want me to be your assistant?"

"Yeah."

"How can I assist you?"

"Easily." Schlossberger took a swig of soup. "First of all, kid, your biggest asset is your ignorance. You're not gonna foul up my mind with any of your ideas like a lot of these wise-ass young punks graduating from Harvard. I don't need no punk security analysts. You'll just follow my orders."

"I'm very good at taking direction, Mr. Schlossberger."

"And I'm good at giving it."

"So far, it seems simple," said Sylvan, digging into his hamburger. "Is there anything else I should know?" "Yeah."

"What is it?"

"How to answer the phone."

"That's easy. I know how to do that. Anything else?"

"Yeah."

"What?"

"How to predict the future."

"Predict the future? I can't do that."

Schlossberger smiled. He put down his soup, leaned forward, and pushed his oily face right under Sylvan's nose. His pockmarked cheeks and assorted collection of moles and wrinkles reminded Sylvan of the moon's surface he had seen on television. "I'm gonna teach you how to predict the future!"

"Really?"

"Yeah. Then I'll teach you how to be a crackerjack broker." Schlossberger leaned back in his chair. "Stick with me, kid. You'll make lotsa dough."

Sylvan beamed enthusiastically. "Sounds great. I've always wanted to read the future. When do we start?"

"We've already started," the broker rumbled, snapping his fingers. A waiter scurried across the floor with the bill. Schlossberger reached into his pocket, pulled out a huge wad, and slapped down

$60.00. "Come on, kid."

They left the restaurant and headed back to the brokerage office. Although the elevator was packed with people, Schlossberger easily shoved his way in, making plenty of room for both himself and his new assistant.

Sylvan was given a desk with a phone on it. Schlossberger handed him a yellow sheet. "Read this report on Gilded Mines Inc. Then call your mother and sell it to her."

"My mother?"

"Yeah. Sell your mother, and you can sell anyone."

"I don't feel good calling my mother about a — "

Schlossberger gave Sylvan a look that would terrify Napoleon. "Call!"

"Okay, okay. Let me read the report."

Sylvan studied the report. Gilded Mines Inc. was a gold mine in California that had been built in 1850 during the gold rush. At the turn of the century, having fallen into disrepair, it was finally destroyed by an underground flood which washed away the support beams. The mine collapsed, killing the six remaining employees in 1912. With the rapid rise in the price of gold, the mine had been reopened under new management. So far, it had produced no gold, but promised a surfeit of the yellow metal in the very near future.

Sylvan tried imagining what Gilded Mines Inc. looked like. A picture of King Midas trying to eat a golden apple flashed through his mind; in the background was the river Pactolus.

He dialed his parents' number.

His mother answered. "Sylvan! I thought you were working today. Is anything wrong?"

"Nothing's wrong, Ma. I'm calling from the brokerage. I'm selling stock and *you* are my first customer."

"Me?"

"Yes, you. Mr. Schlossberger said that if I can sell you a stock, I can sell anybody."

"What! How tasteless! What's the matter with that man? I'm certainly not buying any stupid stock. What kind of business is this, anyway?"

Sylvan heard a click. He turned to Schlossberger. "She hung up."

"Call her again."

"But—"

"Call *her again!*"

"Yes, sir." He dialed again. Again his mother hung up.

"She won't be budged, Mr. Schlossberger. She's not the type to buy stock."

"She'll buy," said Schlossberger. "Nothing happens right away. Sometimes it takes weeks, even months to make a sale. Just keep tryin'."

Suddenly, the phone rang. "Answer it!" Schlossberger commanded.

Sylvan picked up the phone. "Hello ... Ma, is that you?"

"Yes, it is dear. I'm so sorry for the way I spoke to you before," she apologized. "It's just that stocks frighten me; I don't know anything about them. When you tried to sell me one, I thought you were turning against me." She struggled to hold back her sobs. "My own son turning against me. . . ."

"I wasn't turning against you, Ma. I didn't mean anything like that. It's just this is a new job and...."

"Don't say another word, Sylvan. I know it's a new job; and instead of scorning you, yelling at you, and hanging up on you, I should be helping you. I should be buying stock."

Sylvan was speechless. His mother, interpreting his silence as disapproval, sobbed into the phone. "Please, Sylvan, that was a terrible thing for me to do. Please excuse your frightened mother. *Please,* let me buy stock from you."

"Well," Sylvan recovered, "what kind would you like?"

"Any kind at all. Vegetables are best; but, really, it's your choice to make. After all, *you* are the stockbroker."

"You're right, Ma. I think 100 shares of Gilded Mines Inc. would be just right for you."

"That's it. You've always known how I love the Yucatan and the Mayans. Gelted Mayans is just what I want. One hundred shares should be enough for this week."

"Okay, Ma, I'll buy them. Thanks for calling back."

"I'm glad I did it. Thank you for buying so many lovely shares. I'm telling my friends about them. Maybe they'll buy, too."

"That's a good idea, Ma. Do that."

"I will; I will."

"Great. So long now."

Sylvan hung up. Above his head a row of gritty teeth shone under the lights. It was Schlossberger smiling down on him.

The weeks passed. Sylvan was rapidly becoming a crackerjack broker. His soft smooth sales voice—delivered in the sweet tones he had developed during voice lessons at Westman—helped him to increase his accounts dramatically. Many of his first customers were his mother's friends. They bought so many shares of Gilded Mines Inc. that its price was driven up from $1.00 to $7.50 a share. The active and upward movement of the stock caused a stir on Wall Street. Sylvan received calls from brokers in other parts of the country who inquired about the "Eastern Money Combine" that was buying so many shares despite the fact that Gilded Mines had no sales, no earnings, no profits, no income, and even no assets. In fact, it seemed that Gilded Mines Inc. was nothing more than a hole in the company president's backyard.

Months went by. Sylvan forgot about his past life at Westman. The stock market totally consumed him. Stock quotations followed him home after work; at night, after turning off the lights and laying his head on the pillow, ticker tapes rolled through his dreams.

He learned how to answer two phones at once, carry on three simultaneous conversations, promote an unknown company, even how to sell a nonexistent company to an eager speculator. He learned the mechanics of trading not only on the New York, American, and Over-the-Counter Stock Exchanges, but even developed a small following for the infamous Under-the-Counter Exchange, which dealt with negative-income companies selling shares of Hope to very optimistic buyers.

Schlossberger was proud of Sylvan's progress. "You've come a long way, kid," he said one morning.

"Thank you, Mr. Schlossberger."

"Call me Herman."

"All right, Mr. Schlossberger. I'll do that."

"Call me *Herman.*"

Somehow, Sylvan had difficulty picturing Schlossberger as a "Herman." He couldn't say the name easily.

"All right, H-Her. . . ."

"Herman!"

Sylvan finally blurted it out. "Herman." He was amazed to see a big smile forming on his mentor's face.

"I like your work, kid."

"Thank you."

"Thank you, *Herman,*" Schlossberger coached. "Yeah, you've come a long way. I think it's time we had lunch together again."

"That would be fine, *Herman.* The Stockhouse Restaurant?"

"Right. Come by my office at noon."

When they reached the restaurant, Schlossberger and Sylvan sat down by the window overlooking the traffic jam on Broadway. The maitre d' greeted them, and the waiter brought a menu.

"What'll it be?" asked Schlossberger.

"Steak with Mushrooms."

"Good. I'll have the same—and some soup." Schlossberger picked his nose while pushing the menu away. "I've been watching you for the past seven months," he said while his index finger worked its way into the right nostril. "You started out as an ignorant pipsqueak but now you're gettin' a feel for the business." Schlossberger winked. "You're even gettin' a trader's eye. I like that."

Sylvan was moved by the compliment. "I'm glad you're happy with my progress."

"So am I because if I wasn't, you'd have been fired long ago.

The waiter came over, and Schlossberger barked out their orders. Then, leaning towards Sylvan, "Kid, this is a special luncheon. I'm promoting you. From now on, you're going to be an Account Executive."

"Thank you, Mr. Schlos . . . er, Herman. What is an Account Executive?"

"An Account Executive is my assistant."

"But I'm your assistant already."

"Yes, but with the title of Account Executive—AE in the trade—you'll get a raise. I spoke with Schleswig and Holstein the other day. I insisted you were ready for it—and they both agreed."

"That's fantastic."

"Let's drink to it." Schlossberger clinked his soup bowl on Sylvan's water glass. "Now that you're an AE, do you have any questions you'd like to ask me?"

Sylvan thought a moment. "Well," he said slowly, "there is one thing. Many months ago, when we first had lunch here, you said you'd teach me many things about being a broker. One of them was how to predict the future."

"I told you that?"

"Yes. You told me you could predict the future."

"Me?"

"Don't you remember? Even Sam said you could predict it.

"Who's he?"

"Sam, Sam Ferdinand. Oh, never mind about him. But is it true? Can you predict the future?"

Schlossberger grunted strangely; his fingers tapped out an off-beat rhythm on the table. "Yeah, sure I can tell what stocks are gonna do."

Sylvan leaned forward. "You mean, you can predict the future?"

"Sure."

"How?"

"I make it up."

"What do you mean?"

"I make it up as I go along." Schlossberger grunted again, then laughed diabolically. "Customers are always asking me which way a stock is gonna move tomorrow, next week, next year. I got a good imagination. I tell 'em. If I'm right, they think I can predict the future; if I'm wrong, they usually forget about it."

Sylvan sounded disappointed. "There must be more to it than that," he said hopefully.

"There is. The important thing about all this is that I make the decisions for my customers. As long as they don't have to make any decisions on their own, they're happy. If I make a 'mistake' and a stock goes the wrong way . . . they forgive and forget. They won't blame me if I'm wrong 'cause if they do, then *they'll* have to make their own decisions. And that's the last thing they want to do. So I 'predict the future' for them. It gives them peace of mind, and it gives me lots of commissions. We're both happy. It's a good deal."

Sylvan's voice sagged. "So, predicting the future is a lot of bunk."

Schlossberger nodded.

"I guess Sam was wrong."

"Who?"

"He's usually not—"

"Listen, kid, you're hired to make decisions for people about their money. The market is shifting sands; you can't be definite in the market. You gotta stay loose 'cause you never know where you're going or what's gonna happen next. People want answers so they can feel safe. Indecision drives 'em crazy. So, I decide for them. I give 'em answers, even if there aren't any; I make 'em feel safe, even when there's no safety."

Sylvan listened intently. This was a side of Schlossberger he had never seen; it was Schlossberger the philosopher, the psychologist, the man of insight. "You certainly know people," commented our hero admiringly.

"I know my customers."

"You know their feelings, and you know how to handle them when they're afraid."

"Yeah."

"How did you get so wise?"

Schlossberger pounded his chest with the palm of his hand. "I know me!" he proclaimed.

"That's what I'd like to do," said Sylvan.

"What's that?"

Sylvan patted his chest with the inside of his thumb. "Know

me. I wish I could be more decisive, more definite; but I usually feel confused.... Sometimes I just don't know what I want."

"Just like a customer."

"Just like a customer," the young broker agreed. He watched indifferently while the waiter placed the Steak with Mushrooms before both of them. Schlossberger tore off a piece and shoveled it into his mouth.

"How did you get to know yourself so well?" Sylvan asked.

"Therapy."

Sylvan was taken aback. "You're in therapy?" Schlossberger blinked.

"With a shrink ... er, psychiatrist?"

Schlossberger kept chewing. "Psychologist."

"Really?"

"Yup. Been going for three years."

"But, why? You seem so stable."

"Why? Easy. I thought I could predict the future. One day I predicted the market would go up; instead, it collapsed. I knew I was in trouble. I lost lots of customers. When I realized I couldn't predict the future, I fell apart. My wife said 'You'd better see a doctor.' "

Sylvan became pensive. "So, that's how it happened," he said quietly. Then he blurted out, "Maybe that's what I need."

Schlossberger's eyes lit up. "My man's real good."

Sylvan wiped some steak juice off his mouth. "Not so fast. I'm not ready to go yet. But tell me about it. How does it work?"

"Easy as pie. You just go into his office, sit down on the sofa, and say whatever you want."

"That's all?"

"That's all."

"Sounds easy."

"It is easy. But it'll cost you."

"How much?"

"$60.00 an hour."

"Holy cow!"

"And it's not even an hour—it's forty-five minutes."

"That's incredible."

"But it's worth it." Schlossberger beamed; a look of peace and serenity crossed his pockmarked face. His eyes turned blissfully towards the ceiling, as if waiting for a guardian angel to descend and carry him away. "It's worth it," he repeated. "I learn something and get a good rest besides. It soothes my nerves when I see my man."

Sylvan felt jealous. He wished he had someone to soothe his nerves, someone to whom he could say whatever he wanted. Before his eyes, Schlossberger's face was being transformed from a mass of twitching muscles and ticks into a gentle plain of tranquility. As his eyes gazed angelically upward and his vision turned inward, Schlossberger's ugly features actually began to look beautiful. And all this just by *thinking* about his doctor, Sylvan thought. Maybe there was something to this therapy, after all.

"Could you give me his name and phone number?"

Schlossberger took a notebook from his vest pocket, tore out a page, and scribbled: *Dr. Ludwig Lume, 887 Central Park West. Phone: 222-2222.*

Sylvan stuffed the address in his pocket.

Schlossberger drank his soup and finished off his steak in three mouthfuls. Then they toasted "to the future" and called for the bill.

"I predict we're going to pay soon," Sylvan prognosticated.

Schlossberger placed his arm on the young broker's shoulder. "That's the way to predict the future."

They left the restaurant and walked towards the elevator. Minutes later, they were back at their desks answering phone calls.

CHAPTER TEN

Dr. Lume

S YLVAN LOOKED FORWARD TO his first appointment with Dr. Lume. He wondered why he'd been having so many headaches in recent weeks and why he felt tired and depressed. Could the brokerage business be getting to him? Or maybe it was the fights at home with his parents. Perhaps there were unknown motives that needed deep probing to be discovered.

He had an uneasy feeling when he rang the doorbell of Dr. Lume's second floor office. His uneasiness increased when there was no answer. He rang again. No answer. Is today the right day, Sylvan thought. He paced the hall, then rang again. Still no answer. Disappointed, he turned and walked down the stairs. Just as he reached the bottom, a soft voice with a German accent called: "Hello. Hello, down there."

In the doorway stood a short fat man dressed in a bathrobe and slippers; the towel around his neck was the same gray color as the Greek sailor's cap on his head. Thick, wide-rimmed glasses surrounded his pin-ball eyes, which darted back and forth in their sockets like laboratory mice trapped in a cage. His Vandyke was streaked with gray. Cradled within it was a small mouth whose baby-pink lips wiggled as he said, "Hello, hello. Come in, come in."

Sylvan found himself in a vestibule. Abstract paintings and a collection of miniature elephants hung on the wall. The short man motioned towards a bench. *New Yorker* magazines were stacked on top of it. "Sit down," he coaxed, before scampering through a door and disappearing into an adjoining room.

Sylvan sat down, picked up a *New Yorker,* and began leafing through it. After fifteen minutes of reading, he saw a young blonde woman leave the adjoining room. There were tears in her eyes, and she sobbed softly to herself. When she saw Sylvan, she put on her coat and hurried out of the office.

Moments later, the short fat man appeared in the doorway.

"Follow me," he said.

They entered the adjoining room. "Are you Dr. Lume?" Sylvan asked as he sat down on a long leather couch.

The man selected a cigar from his desk drawer, lit it, took a long slow puff, and exhaled upwards. Sylvan's eyes followed the smoke towards the ceiling, where it settled under the recessed lights.

"I am Dr. Lume."

"I like your office," said Sylvan, observing the drawn shades and small Buddha statues on the doctor's desk. "It's very restful here."

"Yes, it's very restful," Lume repeated. His voice was mellow, soothing and soft.

"I think this couch is super. It's so smooth—I've always liked the feel of leather."

"The feel of l e a t h e r...."

Sylvan pointed to the wall. "You sure have a lot of books. Have you read all those books? I mean, all the thick ones?"

Leaning back in his swivel chair, the doctor sent up another cloud of smoke. "Thick ones," he intoned.

"I like to read a lot, too. I like books."

"Books."

"In fact, I love books. I love to read."

"Love?"

"Yes, I love reading. It's a habit I picked up at home. My mother loves reading mysteries, science fiction, that sort of thing. I guess I picked up the habit from my mother."

"Mother?"

"Yes, my mother. My father reads, too, but not that much. He usually falls asleep when he reads a book." "Mother?"

"No, my father. He's the one who falls asleep."

At that moment, Sylvan noticed the padding on the door. His eyes moved to the soundproofed ceiling and heavy brown rug covering the floor.

"How come there's so much padding around here?" he asked, feeling the thickness of the carpet beneath his feet. "Mother?"

"No, padding."

"Padding?"

"Right. Why is there so much padding?"

"Why is there padding," Dr. Lume whispered.

"Yes, why?"

"Because of screaming."

"What screaming?"

"Oh, never mind." Lume turned in his swivel chair. "That is irrelevant. Let us begin. What is your name?"

"It's Sylvan Woods."

"Sylvan Woods?" Dr. Lume looked puzzled. He studied his appointment book. "No, it's 6:30. You must be Jason Grodner."

"I'm Sylvan Woods."

"Strange," muttered the doctor. "Six-thirty is Grodner. Well, no matter. Let us begin. I always like calling my patients by their names. What is your name?"

Sylvan was getting angry. "I already told you—Sylvan Woods."

"Hm . . .what kind of name is that?"

"What do you mean, what kind of name? It's a good name. What kind of name is Lume?"

"It is also a good name, although it is not my real one."

"You changed your name?"

"I changed it from Goldstein in order to hide my past. Before Goldstein, it was Kelly; before that, Bazgakian; before that, Astronovich; and before that . . . I can't even remember."

"You've had many identities."

"It is a doctor's job to have many identities; and to discover the many identities in his patients. Sylvan—if I may call you that—you are many persons. You have many identities. Tell me about some of your identities."

"Me?"

"Yes. Have you ever felt like someone else?"

"Oh, I don't know. . . ."

"Good, good. Lean back, relax. . . . Tell me about it."

"I'm not sure. . . ."

"Yes, go on."

"I feel I have no purpose—not like I used to, anyway."

"Used to?" Lume's eyebrows rose.

"When I was in high school, and even in Westman, I knew what I wanted to be. But, somehow, it all drained out of me.

"Very interesting," Dr. Lume said. "I have written many papers on this drainage problem." He blew another smoke ring towards the ceiling. "And what did you want to be?"

"A musician. A top violinist, to be exact." Sylvan sat up on the couch. "It was all so clear then. My days were all planned, all structured. . . ."

"A musician." The doctor's eyes brightened. "You are a musician.

"I was a musician. Now I'm a stockbroker."

"Aaah, music is wonderful," sighed the doctor.

"Music *was* wonderful. Now everything is kind of drab. When I go home after work, I feel this emptiness inside me; I'm not really committed to anything. I feel like I'm just filling my days with meaningless movement."

"To be able to play the violin is a marvelous thing," the doctor philosophized. "I wish I could play the violin." He put out his cigar and reached for his pipe. Chuckling softly to himself, he said, "Sylvan, I see your problem. You have an obvious gift that you are squandering in the brokerage business. Go back to your music, and your problems will be solved. How lucky you are! I wish I could play the violin."

"Did you ever take lessons?" asked Sylvan.

"Never," Lume answered ruefully.

"Why not?"

The doctor released a long moan. "Can't you see why not?"

"No. Why?"

"Because I'm too short!"

"I don't understand—"

"My fingers are too short."

"That's ridiculous. Let me see your hand."

Sylvan rose from the couch to examine Dr. Lume. Skillfully, he checked out the fatty underside of the doctor's hand; he looked at the stubby fingers, the fleshy thumb, and the sweaty palm; he manipulated each finger segment, studied nails and knuckles, and bent the wrist. "This hand is fine," he concluded. "It is a handsome hand. It will work very well on the violin."

Dr. Lume pulled his hand away. "It is a stubby, disgusting thing! It is too short. What's more, my legs are too short, my arms are too short, my neck is too short; in short, I am too short!"

Sylvan felt sorry for him. "Look, it's really easy to play the violin. Even I could teach you."

Life jumped back into the doctor's eyes. "You could?"

"Sure, there's nothing to it. I'd be glad to show you." Dr. Lume moved to the edge of his chair. "Do you think you could show me now?"

"Sure, whenever you want."

"Wonderful!" Leaping from his seat, Dr. Lume rushed to the closet, opened it, and took an old ply-board violin case down from the shelf. "It's been up here for years," he said, dusting the case with his sleeve. He placed it carefully on his desk. "I've never dared use it before. You've given me hope. Maybe I can learn to play, after all."

Dr. Lume's fingers trembled as he opened the case. "Can you tune it?" he asked, handing it to Sylvan.

Sylvan tightened the bow. Glancing through the F hole, he saw the torn *Made in Brooklyn* label glued inside with rubber cement. Dr. Lume's face beamed with childlike rapture while Sylvan put the violin under his chin and tuned the ancient strings.

The doctor stamped his feet excitedly. "Beautiful, beautiful! I can't wait to start!"

"You can't play the violin in a swivel chair," Sylvan instructed. "Your bow arm has to be free. It would be better for you to sit here," he patted the couch, "on a stable support."

Dr. Lume moved to the couch. Sylvan sat down in the doctor's swivel chair and said, "Before we begin, tell me about yourself. I want to know your background and how you became interested in music."

"Of course," Lume answered, trying to restrain his eagerness. "You must know that." He leaned back, propped his head against a pillow and tried to remember.

"It all began when I was a little boy. Jascha was my best friend and his parents gave him a violin for his birthday. Two weeks later, he started taking lessons."

"How did that make you feel?"

Dr. Lume turned his face towards the wall. "Terrible, just terrible. I wanted a violin, too. I wanted to learn how to play. I begged my parents for lessons, but they said, 'Ludwig, you are too short to play the violin. Run along and play with your toy bombs.' Can you imagine that? What kind of warped parents tell a child such things? My parents were dull-witted nincompoops, and I often told them this, even at the early age of four."

Dr. Lume began patting the leather sofa with his palms. "But what did they know? They kept saying, 'Children the likes of you don't play musical instruments. Leave us alone. Shut up! Go play with your bombs!' I knew then that the power of music was greater than any bomb; it was a secret weapon that made bombs look like peanuts. At that moment, I fell in love with music. I began to worship music; I knelt before the Muse of Harmony who would help me overcome my smallness and make me feel powerful and great. On that day, the war between myself and my parents began." Lume gritted his teeth. "Their weapon was abuse; mine was my *wish* that someday I might play the violin and through my playing become *Master of the World!*"

Dr. Lume's eyes gleamed.

"Did you ever take any violin lessons?" Sylvan asked again.

"Never, never. I was too afraid of the power I might unleash.

Aah, the violin . . . the very thought of it makes me ecstatic."

"Growing up like that must have been hard on you," Sylvan said sympathetically. "Perhaps I can help you."

"I hope so." There was a note of desperation in the doctor's voice.

Sylvan pushed the violin under Lume's chin and tilted his head slightly to the right. "Draw the bow gently across the strings," he instructed.

Lume did what he was told. A terrible scraping sound filled the room.

"Press *gently* on the strings," Sylvan suggested.

Lume tried again and produced a bone-chilling horror reminiscent of a death rattle. He put down the violin and almost wept. "My fingers are too short! I knew it, I knew it!"

"Don't despair," Sylvan coaxed. "It takes years to master the violin. You're giving up after the first few minutes."

Lume hung his head. "You're right. Shame on me. Should I try again?"

"Of course. Try again—and again and again. Never give up.

The doctor lifted the violin to his chin once more. Soon he was creating such a screech that Sylvan wished he would give up. Our hero protected himself by sticking his fingers in his ears. He was saved from further torture only by an alarm that went off on the doctor's desk signaling the end of the session.

"This has been excellent therapy," said Dr. Lume, putting his violin back in its case. "My fee is $60.00 payable at the end of each session. I accept only cash."

CHAPTER ELEVEN

Another Session

WELCOME TO LUME'S CASTLE!" Thus did Dr. Lume welcome Sylvan into his Long Island home on a day when therapy could not take place in his Manhattan office due to a transit, sanitation, and police strike.

Crossing the threshold, he heard Beethoven's "Pastoral" coming through the heating system. The sound was so distorted Sylvan mistook it for the "Rite of Spring." Looking around the living room, he saw hundreds of records and record jackets strewn haphazardly in corners or piled on chairs and coffee tables. Cellophane record sleeves served to plug holes in the window panes; the rug was patterned after a photograph of Artur Rubinstein on a record jacket.

"Where do we have our session?" Sylvan asked, sitting down in the armchair whose arm rests tapered into a likeness of Chopin.

Dr. Lume opened his arms in a gesture of total acceptance. "What better place than here, surrounded by the *sound* of great music." He pointed to the floor. "Lie down on the rug. I will sit on the sofa. Let us begin."

"But shouldn't we start with your violin lesson?"

"Do you feel more secure with that format?" asked Dr. Lume, wisely employing the Socratic method.

"We always start with your lesson," answered Sylvan defensively.

"True. But this format has put you in control. You have too much control, Sylvan. I am going to take away your control."

"But I came to give you a lesson—"

"That will not happen today."

Sylvan stamped on the floor. "I'm paying a lot of money for this damned therapy," he shouted. "I didn't come here to lie on the rug. I came to give you a lesson—and I will!"

Lume was unperturbed. "There will be no lesson today." Sylvan pointed to the violin case leaning against the sofa.

"Get your violin immediately!" he commanded.

"I will not."

"You will!"

"No. Today is your turn, young man." Sylvan was getting nervous. Lume was right. The lessons had given him a sense of security, a feeling of control, and even power over the doctor. By teaching, he had managed to avoid his own problems. Without his teaching prop, he felt vulnerable and helpless.

"I don't know what to say," Sylvan pleaded.

Dr. Lume lit his pipe, sat back on the sofa, and sent a long curl of smoke towards the ceiling. "Say whatever comes to mind."

"I need a script."

"Nonsense. I thought you were so good at improvising."

"I was, once. . .but I lost it."

"Aaaah, a lost love. Tell me about it."

"It's dead. There's really nothing to say."

"The dead have a way of rising."

"I'd prefer they stay dead."

"Nothing stays dead forever, and nothing lives forever," the doctor reflected. "It's all part of a cycle. Long ago, you were able to improvise. Now you can't perform without a script. Those are two sides of the same person. Today the script is dominant. But improvisation is not dead—only temporarily asleep." Lume's voice hardened. "Time to wake up your improvisation. Do it now! Say whatever comes to mind."

"I'm afraid to do that."

"Why? "

"I might say something terrible."

"Like what? What would you say?"

"Are you kidding? If you think I'd tell you what's *really* on my mind, you'd better think again."

"Come, come, Sylvan. Don't be defensive. I know it's difficult, even painful. But, you are here to understand yourself, to reveal and overcome your doubts and deepest fears. Relax.... Let your mind wander. . . . Tell me, what is the first thought that comes into your mind?"

"I want to kill you."

"What!"

"It would be a slow death."

Dr. Lume straightened; his face flushed. "You want to kill me! How dare you talk to me that way!"

"But you ask me to tell you the first thought that came into my mind—"

"You should have picked the second."

"I didn't mean to frighten you," Sylvan said, a bit startled. "Come. I think a violin lesson will soothe you."

Dr. Lume regained his poise. "You're right. We need a break."

He rose, walked quickly to his violin case, took out the violin, and fondled it lovingly.

"Put it under your chin," Sylvan said. "That's it. Hold your bow arm higher. . . . Good. Good!"

Agonizing minutes later Lume said, "I feel much better now." He put the violin back in its case, sat on the couch, and lit his pipe. "Now, tell me the *second* thought that comes into your mind."

Sylvan thought a moment. "I just feel confused, vulnerable—kind of lost."

"That is good," Dr. Lume reassured him. "Feeling vulnerable can open your mind to new experiences. You may be getting ready to explore another side of yourself."

"Since I lost music, I've felt abandoned. Nothing has come along to replace it."

"I understand. Music is a great love. But what exactly do you feel? What have you lost?"

A long silence followed as Sylvan retraced his life since graduation. What had he lost? Was it his certainty of purpose, his definition of self?

"I've lost my desire to play the violin, that's for sure."

"You just put your finger on it," said the doctor.

"Finger on what?"

"On the reason you feel lost and empty."

"Is it because I lost my desire to play the violin?"

"Not that you have lost your desire to play the violin; rather, you have lost your desire to *play*."

"Play?"

"Yes, play. Being able to play is one of the most important things anyone can do." Dr. Lume patted his chest proudly. "When my patients learn how to play—I release them. I say, don't bother me with your problems anymore. If you can play, your problems will go away by themselves. In fact, the problem with most people is they cannot play; or rather, they have *for-*

gotten how to play."

"Aw, playing is for kids," Sylvan argued. "Adults don't do that."

Dr. Lume's voice became philosophical. "Sylvan, life is a great riddle. But, when we speak of enjoyment or fulfillment, one of the strangest things about it is: Whatever is useful is useless, and whatever is practical is impractical."

"What's that mumbo-jumbo supposed to mean?"

"Precisely this: Useful things are *means* to achieve some end. Playing is good because it is an *end* in itself. Most people want to earn money because they hope someday they can relax and enjoy it; they hope that someday they will be able to play. The reason you practice scales and exercises on the violin is because you hope to eventually *play* the violin. You see this even in your business—the stock market. People don't work the stock market; they *play* it."

A glimmer of light shone in Sylvan's eyes. "It is fun to play," he conceded. "I wish I could still do it."

Dr. Lume consoled him. "You'll do it again. It just takes time to undo the knots of your past."

"I used to love playing the violin," Sylvan recalled. "Sometimes, I got so involved, I forgot the music and just improvised."

"Improvising is the highest form of play."

"But why can't I improvise? Why can't I play anymore?"

"Fear."

"Fear?"

"Yes. Fear kills fun; it kills play. Fear kills the desire and the ability to improvise."

"But what do I have to be afraid of?"

"That is what you are here to find out."

Sylvan looked hopefully at Dr. Lume. "Are you saying that if

I conquer my fears, I'll be able to improvise and play again?"

The doctor nodded.

"And the lost feeling will go away?"

"It will."

"And all I have to do is find out what I'm afraid of."

"That's all. But that's a lot."

"Well, let's get started then. What am I afraid of?"

"Yes, what *are* you afraid of?"

"I'm afraid to say."

"Of course."

The dialogue stopped. Silence cloaked the room while Sylvan searched his mind. Finally, he asked, "I'm afraid of my mother?"

"Don't ask me, tell me!"

"I'm afraid of my mother."

"Is that true?"

"I don't know."

"Then why did you tell it to me?"

"Being afraid of your mother is a good answer," Sylvan confessed. "I thought it would make you happy."

"So, you're trying to please me."

"Well. . . ."

"Your basic desire is to make me happy."

"I hadn't thought of it that way. Yes, I suppose so."

"You want to make me, your audience, happy."

"Yes."

"What about you? Does that answer please you?" Sylvan was about to answer when the alarm went off, terminating the session.

"Time's up," said Lume abruptly.

"Must we end so suddenly?" asked Sylvan, somewhat annoyed. "I was just getting warmed up."

"We must end now," answered the doctor. "Besides, what's the difference? It's all process, anyway."

Sylvan thought a great deal about the "process" as he sat on the subway riding home.

During the next few months Sylvan's brain was remodeled; he learned to symbolically yell at his mother, beat up his father, and scream over a missing button; or cry over comments like "How are you?" Therapy helped him deal with his fears of failure, success, and freedom. And as his fears fell away, he found himself thinking about music again.

One afternoon when Sylvan entered the office, Lume cheerfully suggested: "We should go to a concert together."

"That sounds strange."

"It is strange," Lume agreed. "But it will be good for you. I want to study your reactions to the music."

"Will you pay for the tickets?"

Dr. Lume reached into his pocket and pulled out two stubs. "I've already paid for these. The Amsterdam Philharmonic is playing an all-Beethoven program next Wednesday night in Carnegie Hall."

After the session, he ushered Sylvan to the door. "See you at 7:30 in front of the box office."

Sylvan walked out. He nodded hello to the next patient—a blond woman in tears—put on his coat, and headed down the stairs.

CHAPTER TWELVE

Beethoven

SYLVAN THOUGHT ABOUT HIGH school and his many hours of violin practice as he boarded the Seventh Avenue subway on his way to Carnegie Hall. Walking up the stairs at the 57th Street station brought back memories of symphonies, soloists, and choral works he had heard. The line of music lovers waiting for tickets outside the box office reminded him of the hours he had waited to hear Jascha Heifetz, Pablo Casals, Eugene Ormandy. . . . He remembered the cold winter evenings when eager concertgoers queued up in their overcoats while a bearded fiddler, his gloves cut off at the finger tips so he could feel the strings, played for them. The old man's violin case lay open on the sidewalk and Sylvan had thrown pennies and nickels into it. He had often wondered if violinists who did not practice ended up playing in front of Carnegie Hall, rather than inside it.

He met Dr. Lume at the box office, and, tickets in hand, they marched past the line of music fans, through the main entrance, and up to the second floor mezzanine where first-row seats overlooking the orchestra awaited them. It was the most expensive seat Sylvan had ever been in. He was pleased with his wonderful view of the stage.

Dr. Lume adjusted his thick glasses and surveyed the seats behind them. "I like to sit close," he said. "I like to *see* the music, as well as hear it."

"That's a very poetic idea."

"Poetic?" Lume sneered. "By 'poetic,' do you mean it is unreal?"

Sylvan laughed. "Well . . . er, yes. You *hear* notes; you don't see them."

"I see them! Why do you think I always wear my glasses to a concert?" Lume waved his arms like a conductor leading a symphony. "Sylvan, you are a silly boy. Everyone in his right mind knows that notes are *things*. Notes can fly; notes can speak; notes can touch and feel. And let me tell you one thing you should always remember: Each note is the living spirit of some departed soul. It resides temporarily in a human body. When the body dies, the note, in the form of a spirit, escapes and floats through space. Each lonely note is like an orphan looking for a home. Once the music starts, I *see* these lonely notes flying around the hall. I see many of my departed patients here, and pick up many new ones besides."

Dr. Lume removed his overcoat, hung it over the railing, and sat down. Sylvan was surprised to see him wearing a black tuxedo, a starched white shirt with a high collar and bow tie, and black polished shoes.

"Why are you dressed so formally?" he asked.

"What makes you say such a thing? I am not dressed formally. This is my *normal* dress for a concert. I respect the Spirit of the Music. The question is, why are you dressed so badly. You don't wear dungarees and a sweatshirt to a concert. Where's your respect?"

"Just asking," said Sylvan. "I didn't mean to offend you.

"You didn't offend me; you offended the music!"

They sat down. The crowd streamed into Carnegie Hall. Soon, every seat was taken. The orchestra members appeared on stage. Sylvan saw the lights dim and heard a hush descend upon the audience. Applause greeted the conductor as he walked out. He bowed and mounted the podium. His well-formed bald head shone under the spotlight, and his tuxedo tails flapped as he raised his arms. The musicians raised their instruments. The downbeat was given and the melodic opening of Beethoven's Pastoral filled the open space.

The orchestra played beautifully—each note perfectly in place. the dynamics tastefully executed, and the tone rich and wonderful.

After nearly ten minutes of these divine melodies, Sylvan heard a peculiar disturbance on his left. Dr. Lume, obviously transported by the music, was grunting and swaying back and forth.

"Dr. Lume," Sylvan whispered, gently touching his elbow. "Please, be quiet."

Lume kept grunting, oblivious to his patient's request. Sylvan squeezed his elbow and spoke into his ear. "Why are you doing that?"

"I am riding the waves," the doctor intoned like a Hindu mystic one step away from Nirvana. "The Music transports me to a Higher Reality. I am merging into the Transcendent Being—the part of me I like best." Lume stared directly at his guest. "Now, shut up and leave me alone!"

Sylvan retreated; he tried concentrating on the music. Lume continued making animal sounds. Grunting, heavy breathing, gurgles, and growls spilled from his mouth. His swaying increased until the whole row of seats was rhythmically rocking to his movements. As the music rose in crescendo, he began beating the railing in front of him, stamping his feet, and salivating.

"Be quiet!" commanded the man sitting behind him.

"Ssh!" hissed a chorus of matrons from across the aisle.

"Sir, we are trying to listen!" explained a young Juilliard graduate through clenched teeth.

Lume paid no attention to the complaints. "Ah, Beethoven, you wondrous creature," he sighed aloud as he stood up and raised his palms to the sky. "Beethoven, Beethoven, you are truly a god! What suffering! What pain! What beauty!"

"You're the pain!" shouted the Juilliard graduate, angrily waving his music score. His teeth no longer clenched; rather, his mouth was wide open hurling abuses upon Dr. Lume. "You barbarian slob! Sit down and shut up!"

"Ssh, quiet," repeated the matrons. "Please *sit down!*" Calls from the back resounded through the Hall: "Down in front! *Down in front!*"

Lume climbed on his seat and continued calling forth his invisible deity: "Blow ye horns! Blast ye trumpets! Bring in the Lord of Music! Beethoven! Beethoven! We fall on our knees before you! Sing, sing, oh, you master of suffering strings! Cry on your violin! Weep, weep, ye wounded woodwinds!" Tears were streaming down his cheeks.

One of the security guards came running down the aisle, followed by two policemen. Taking Lume firmly by the arm, he said with quiet authority, "Come with me."

"I will not!" Dr. Lume tore his arm away. "Beethoven, Beethoven," he wailed.

He was still wailing "Beethoven!" when the guards lifted him out of his seat, carried him up the aisle, and deposited him outside Carnegie Hall on the corner of Fifty-seventh Street.

Sylvan stayed to the end of the concert. He went home alone.

CHAPTER THIRTEEN

Cured

ONTHS PASSED. SYLVAN CONTINUED his weekly therapy sessions. They fell into a familiar pattern: During the first half-hour, he gave Dr. Lume a violin lesson; the second half-hour was devoted to Sylvan's emotional problems. The sessions always ended with the alarm ringing, and the doctor extending his palm, saying, "Honorarium, please," or more simply, "Where's my money?"

Sylvan explored many unknown facets of himself. He found out why he was angry with his father for sleeping so much; why his mother threw temper tantrums when he didn't pick up his socks; why Sam's directiveness had been so important to him; and why he was losing interest in the brokerage business. But the basic question still remained unanswered:

Why had he given up the creative life? In this, he made scant progress. In short, he was as lost as he had been when he first entered Dr. Lume's office over a year ago.

Therefore, he was surprised when, at the end of a dull session, Dr. Lume said, "Sylvan, you have made great progress since the first day you came to me."

"By 'progress,' do you mean that my problems have become greater?" Sylvan asked.

"No, no, not at all," Lume laughed. "Your problems have diminished. You have progressed in the conquest of your fears and doubt. . . . And I have progressed on the violin. Since our sessions began, my technique has improved to the point where I can play Mozart Sonatas without missing a note. My feelings of inferiority about short fingers, short arms, short legs, my worries about my shortcomings all have been cut short." Lume patted his chest with satisfaction.

"That's nice to hear, Doctor," Sylvan said, "but what about me?"

Lume looked surprised. "You?"

"Yes. What about my problems?"

"Your problems? How did your problems get into this?"

"I didn't mean to interrupt you," Sylvan apologized. "I know how important the violin is to you. But what about my worries and anxieties. You know, the ones I came to see you with originally."

"Ha, ha!" Dr. Lume leaned back in his swivel chair, smiling. "Don't worry about them, my friend. They'll go away in time. And don't feel too badly about interrupting me. It doesn't bother me at all. I just feel so good today!" A radiant smile lit his face. "In fact, would you believe, I have made so much progress on the violin this year, that even my stage fright has diminished to the point where I have finally decided to give my first public *concert!*"

"Oh, no!"

"Oh, yes. Yesterday, I called Carnegie Recital Hall to arrange my debut."

"What! You booked Carnegie Recital Hall? You?"

"Unfortunately, the Hall's schedule has been filled for the entire year, so I could not get it. However, I certainly didn't want to wait until next year; I might forget all I've learned by then. I need to give a concert now. Consequently, I made arrangements for my debut to be given in the auditorium of P.S. 101 in Queens. I'm playing three Mozart Sonatas and two scales. Would you like to come?"

"But, Dr. Lume, you're not ready for a concert. You can hardly hold the instrument correctly."

"That is ridiculous, Sylvan. What difference does it make how I hold it, as long as I can hold it."

"Yes, but when you play, it sounds so terrible."

"And who are *you* to say that?"

"I'm your teacher."

"My teacher? Ha! You are not my teacher. You are my patient. You merely helped me clear up a few technical problems before I could discover the qualities in myself which I can now express in my music. But no matter—that is not what I wanted to talk to you about."

"What did you want to talk to me about?"

"Sylvan, you have made substantial progress here. You came in as a frightened tadpole. You are now a frightened frog. You have graduated. Congratulations! It is my professional opinion that you are cured."

"Cured of what?"

"A silly question. I will not even bother answering it. Let me say simply that you no longer need therapy. Your therapy sessions with me are over. I pronounce you . . . done!" Dr. Lume waved his arms over Sylvan like a magic wand.

"But, I don't *feel* cured, Dr. Lume; I still need therapy," Sylvan stuttered. "Please, don't dismiss me. I have more problems. Really, I do."

"Now, now, don't beg," Dr. Lume answered in an understanding tone. "I know how threatening it is to know you're cured; I know how lonely it must feel without dilemmas."

"I'll have *more* problems if I don't come to see you."

"Ridiculous! You can't cling to me forever."

"But, Dr. Lume," Sylvan said. "Where will I go? What will I do without your guidance? What's more, what will *you* do without *mine*? *You* can't even play your scales in tune yet."

"That is kind of you, Sylvan, to think of my needs," Lume answered. "However, as for my scales, they have developed to a degree I would never have dreamed possible to achieve. My self-confidence in violin-playing has grown tremendously—to the point where I no longer need you."

"That's not possible."

"No, it's true. I can get along fine on my own."

"Well, maybe you can, but I can't."

"You can. And you will. Besides, I am raising my fees next week. I know you can't afford them."

There was a long pause.

"I guess I *would* save money by not seeing you," Sylvan pondered aloud.

"Indeed. And as I raise my fees, you will be saving even more money. Think on the positive side."

Just then, the alarm rang, ending the session.

"I hate to leave so abruptly," Sylvan whined. "Can't we—"

"Time to go," Dr. Lume answered curtly.

"But—"

"Time to move into the world and make your mark." Dr. Lume glanced down at his wristwatch. "And, if you can't move into the world, at least leave my office."

"Dr. Lume, do you have any last words for me, any final advice?"

"I do."

Sylvan listened intently. "What?"

"Get out!"

"Dr. Lume—"

But the good healer had stood up, raised his arm, and was pointing his index finger to the door. "Go!" he cried, in a most unwavering voice.

Sylvan reached into his pocket, paid Dr. Lume, and terminated his therapy.

The Search
Continues

CHAPTER FOURTEEN

On the Road Again

SYLVAN FELT LOST WHEN he left Dr. Lume's office. Where would he go? What would he do? Who would lead him through the maze of dead-end directions that, for the moment, was his life?

But as the days passed, these feelings subsided. A new sense of adventure grew within him. He was free of therapy's constant introspection, free to run away from his problems—or, at least, look for new ones.

Perhaps he just needed time to think. After all, therapy had helped give him a new sense of self, and his work at the brokerage had widened his financial horizons. He needed to assimilate these changes.

He passed small shops and a newsstand as he walked down the street. The wind blew newspapers and Styrofoam cups along the sidewalk.

Maybe it was time to leave the country again. Travel. Yes, that was it! His stride quickened. Where would he go? Europe, Asia, Africa, China, Idaho—he could go anywhere.

He had enough money saved up to keep going for at least a

year. It all felt right. Time to give up the safe and secure—time to take the gamble, plunge into the unknown.

He hurried to a pay phone to call Schlossberger. "Herman, I need a leave of absence."

"Lume's gotten to ya," Schlossberger grunted.

"Yes. I've got to get away to think things over."

"Leave of absence, huh?"

"Right."

"What about all these orders you're gettin', all these commissions?"

"I'll just have to let them go."

"What about me? I made you what you are today."

"I know, and I'm grateful. Still, I need to get away." Sylvan held the phone away from his ear as expletives followed.

Finally, his mentor said, "I can't give you a leave of absence."

"Why not?"

"I don't do things that way." There was a pause. "But I'll tell you what *I can* give you."

"What's that?"

"A permanent leave."

Sylvan hesitated. He hadn't wanted to cut his ties permanently. He considered it, then realized there was no other choice.

"Sold," he exclaimed.

"Okay," Schlossberger growled. "You got a deal. Write me a letter on French stocks."

"You bet I w i l l.   .   . . Herman, I hope you're not mad-" Sylvan heard a definitive click. As he hung up the phone, he knew another link had been severed.

He left the booth and walked toward the Seventh Avenue subway. On his right, sandwiched between a bakery and a shoe store, was a small travel agency. The window was covered with posters, fliers, and brochures, all attesting to the benefits of travel. A sign, *Travel Yes, Travail No,* hung from a chai above the doorway.

Sylvan entered. A woman in a business suit greeted him with a smile.

Sylvan introduced himself. "I want to go someplace, but I don't know where."

"You've come to the right place," she said, pointing to the brochures that lay scattered across her desk. "Here are a few places you might consider. Go the traditional route by visiting England, France, Germany, Spain, or Italy. . . . Or if you're looking for something different, try Turkey, Greece, Russia, Brazil—or Ireland."

"They all sound good," Sylvan said, fingering through the pile of brochures, "but I'd like a place that's *very* different."

The agent thought a moment. "Very different?" She sat down at her desk, glanced through some brochures in a drawer, then rose. "I know just the place: Bulgaria!"

"Bulgaria?"

"Yes, Bulgaria."

"Where's Bulgaria?"

"It's in Eastern Europe. Its golden beaches are on the Black Sea; the Rhodope Mountains are believed to be the most romantic in Europe; there are plains, rivers, and peasant villages filled with folk culture. Westerners hardly ever go there. In fact, most people don't even know where Bulgaria is."

"I'm one of them. Do you have any brochures?"

"Brochures on Bulgaria?" she laughed. "There are no brochures on Bulgaria. Simply finding the country is an adventure in its own right."

"That's what I need," Sylvan said, "an adventure. I want to get as far from everything as possible."

"You can't get much further than Bulgaria," the agent offered. She walked over to Sylvan. "Young man, I'm stepping out for awhile. Even though I *know* this trip is right for you, I want to give you time to make up your own mind. Think it over. But I'm sure that as soon as I walk through that door, you will have decided on Bulgaria."

"Suppose I have some questions?" Sylvan called after her.

"We'll handle questions later," she replied. "When planning an adventure of any kind, it is best to find solitude. Leaving you here alone to think is a service I provide for my customers."

"I've always dreamed of sailing on the *Ile de France,*" Sylvan's father said wistfully.

"Sylvan, did you pack your aspirins?" his mother asked.

"No, Ma," he answered as he watched the dock workers loading cargo on the ships bound for foreign ports. Lines of taxis transported passengers to their ships; international flags flew in the harbor; he heard foreign accents and foreign languages around him. His mind was already on its way to Bulgaria.

His mother shook him. "What's the matter with you? Why didn't you bring them? What will happen if you get a headache?"

"Stop worrying about Sylvan," his father broke in. "He's twenty-four years old. He can take care of himself. Besides, they have aspirins in Europe too."

Sylvan touched his mother's arm. "I don't need aspirins anymore, Ma. Dr. Lume cured my headaches. He showed what caused them."

"And what is their cause?" his mother asked.

"I don't want to go into that now," Sylvan answered. "Let's just say I can handle them. That's what counts. Don't worry."

She pulled an envelope out of her pocketbook and handed it to her son. "Sam wanted to gay goodbye personally, but he couldn't make it, so he wrote you this note."

Sylvan opened the envelope:

> *Dear Sylvan,*
>
> *Sorry I can't be with you on this day of your departure, but business—my Music School—prevents me from leaving.*
>
> *If you have a chance, look up Penko Dardanovich. He's an old friend of mine from conservatory days; he lives in Sofia, where he is head of the Sofia Sanitation Department. I think he will be helpful to you. He loves music and plays an excellent cello. His address is: 4 Rilko Street (Uliza Rilko), Sofia.*
>
> > *With affection,*
> > *Sam*

Sylvan put the letter in his pocket. "Thanks, Ma. This is just what I need—a contact in Bulgaria."

"We'd better board now," his father urged. "It's getting late."

They walked up the staircase on the side of the ship. "Where is Room 46?" Sylvan asked a porter. Following his pointed finger, the trio entered a narrow hall.

"Here it is," Sylvan's mother exclaimed. The door creaked as she pushed it open. A bed-light screwed into the wall illuminated double berths, an armchair, and a desk nailed to the floor.

"Jesus, this room is like a coffin," piped his father.

"A coffin for two," came a voice from the upper berth. Sylvan stepped over to the mound underneath the blankets. "Nice to meet you," he said.

The blankets moved. "You're interrupting my sleep."

"Sorry."

"The world is full of sorrows," the voice moaned. The blankets lifted, revealing an angular face with sunken cheeks and hollowed eyes. Sylvan's roommate threw a pair of gangly legs over the side of the bed. "Are you all moving in?" he asked.

"No, no," Mr. Woods said, "only Sylvan. We're leaving right away."

"Good."

Sylvan extended his hand. "Glad to meet you."

His roommate did not shake the proffered hand but, rather, observed it, like a scientist scrutinizing a fish. Sylvan lowered it slowly. "What's your name?"

"I'll remain nameless."

"Nameless, eh? Is that your first name?"

"Oh, never mind, you thick-wit. I'm Larry Gussman. My friends call me Ludo."

"Do you have any friends?"

"That's a terrible thing to say, Sylvan," his mother chided. "Where are your manners?"

"Ludo is a strange nickname," Sylvan's father observed. Ludo glared at Sylvan's father. "It means 'crazy' in Bulgarian."

"Well, I like your *regular* name very much," Mrs. Woods said. "We know a conductor named Vladimir Gussman. He helped our Sylvan a great deal when he was a violinist. We liked him very much."

Ludo climbed back into bed without a word, pulled the blankets over his head, and snored so loudly that Sylvan's father suggested they all leave the cabin.

"Will you be happy with that snorer?" his mother asked when they were outside the door.

"Don't worry, Ma. I'll be fine."

"Don't forget to write."

"I'll write you every month."

"Every week," his mother insisted.

"Every month." He hugged his parents and gave them both a goodbye kiss.

Sylvan reentered his cabin, which sounded like the inner chambers of a tuba with Ludo snoring.

"They're gone now. You can get up."

Ludo's head popped out from under the blankets. "Good. I hate parents."

"Mine aren't too bad."

"I hate parents," Ludo repeated.

"Why?"

"Never mind."

Sylvan put his suitcase on the bed. "Do you know Vladimir Gussman?" he asked. "He's a great conductor. I performed the Mendelssohn Violin Concerto with his orchestra when I was in high school. He helped me a lot."

"He never helped me."

"Why should he have helped you?"

"He's my father."

"Your *father!*"

"Yes."

"So you *are* related."

"He's my father, but we're *not* related!"

"What do you mean?"

"I wouldn't call that creep any relation of mine."

Sylvan felt embarrassed by this sudden contact with Vladimir Gussman's personal life. Evidently, the high standards Gussman demanded in music didn't carry over to family relationships.

"Didn't you like growing up surrounded by music?"

On the word "music," Ludo leaped out of bed. His size-fourteen shoes landed with a resounding thud in front of Sylvan, who found himself staring directly into Ludo's shoulder. Ludo was seven feet tall!

"Don't ever mention that word again!" Ludo howled. "What word?"

"*That* word."

"You mean 'music'?"

"Stop! Stop! I can't stand it!" Ludo put his hands over his ears.

"That's the word, eh?"

Ludo nodded. His eyes were wild.

"Okay. I won't say it again."

Ludo looked relieved.

"It must have been hard growing up with someone so committed to—er, *it,*" Sylvan said gently.

Ludo took a ping-pong ball out of his pocket and squeezed it between his fingers. "*Horrible.* All he ever thought about was his damn instruments. He couldn't even remember my name! He called me 'Piano.' 'Larry! Larry!' I yelled. 'My name is Larry!' But he never listened. One day my mother fell on her knees begging him to remember my name. It must have made an impression because after that he called me 'Bassoon.' It drove me crazy. To this day, I have trouble remembering my name. Whenever I introduce myself, I grind my teeth to keep from forgetting who I am. That's why I've had so many dental problems, so many fallen teeth."

"Fallen teeth?"

"Yes. It's a rare dental abnormality caused by depression.

"I've never heard of it."

"Not many people have. It occurs when your life is so depressing that even your gums give you no support. Under such conditions, the teeth lean backwards, or 'fall' towards the tongue. The correlation between falling teeth and the chronically depressed is a new field in dentistry."

"You sure know a lot about teeth."

"That's my field."

"You're a dentist?"

Ludo wiped his molars with his finger to emphasize his point. "Have been for three years."

"I never would think you're a dentist."

"Oh, yes. I've already made important contributions to the field."

A whistle sounded.

"The ship's leaving," Sylvan said excitedly. "Let's go on deck and wave goodbye to America."

The young men ran down the hall and up the spiral stair-case. On deck the sun was shining; waves slapped against the ship.

"Goodbye, America. Goodbye, old life!" Sylvan shouted, waving to the crowd on the pier.

The *Ile de France* pulled out of the harbor. New York City faded into the distance.

The rhythmic rocking and endless fields of water quickly affected Sylvan's mind. Memories of the brokerage business and the rapid pace of city life disappeared. New thoughts filtered in. Dreams of the future rose before him.

CHAPTER FIFTEEN

Ping-Pong

UNDER A SIGN READING *Game Room* stood a ping-pong table. Ludo was talking to a squat man; they nodded in agreement. Sylvan came over as the two men walked to opposite sides of the table.

Ludo was the first to serve. His mouth twitched as he raised the ball above his head. A loud crack—and the ball disappeared.

"Come on, serve it," shouted the squat man.

"I did." Ludo pointed to the wall behind his opponent. "It's over there."

"Oh," grunted the man, turning to retrieve it.

On the next serve, Ludo cut the ball so sharply it jumped from the right side of the table to the left. His opponent lunged for it, missed it, and fell flat on the table.

"Point two," Ludo said, wiping his teeth. He prepared for his next serve by holding his paddle parallel to the floor and pushing it back and forth. His opponent crouched, and moved from side-to-side, anticipating Ludo—certain the ball would go to the right, but just then Ludo switched hands and shot a left-handed serve past him.

The man looked stunned.

Ludo beat him 11-0.

By then, a crowd of onlookers had gathered around the table. "Anyone want to play?" he asked, running the rubber of his paddle over his teeth.

"Go get him, Sammy," urged voices from the crowd.

Sammy, a lanky, middle-aged man with a close-cropped head of white hair, waved them away. "Not now," he answered.

"Come on, Sammy. You can take him," the crowd insisted.

Sammy smiled confidently. "Encourage me."

As if responding on cue, the crowd chanted: "Sammy, Sammy, Whammy, Whammy." The more they chanted, the more Sammy smiled.

The woman next to Sylvan said, "Sammy used to be a pro. Now he's in real estate."

Finally, Sammy decided to play. He picked up the paddle, examined it, and walked to the ping-pong table.

"Ready?" Ludo asked.

"Ready," Sammy answered. His eyes narrowed as he crouched.

Ludo started with his "Broadway Seventh Avenue" serve. Sammy returned it easily.

Ludo was so surprised, he missed the ball.

"So, you want to play like that!" he shouted, and laid on his "Sliced Egg" serve—a backhand slice followed by a fore-hand slice, completed before the ball hit the table.

Sammy returned that one, too. Again Ludo missed.

Ludo's face was turning purple. He straightened to his full seven feet and delivered his "Infantry" serve—the ball simply marched across the net.

Sammy returned it easily; but this time, Ludo smashed the ball with such force that it flew past him, through an open window, crossed the deck, and almost went overboard.

"Point one," said Ludo, wiping his teeth.

From then on, the game was fierce. Ludo served screwball serves. Sammy deftly returned them, adding his own slams, twists, and cuts. The ball moved like lightning between them. They battled eye-to-eye, or standing ten feet in back of the table, smashing long drives across the net, or running to the corners retrieving shots that would have been sure points in any other game.

The crowd loved it. They shouted encouragement. The score see-sawed back and forth. At last Ludo needed only one point to win. Both players stood fifteen feet behind the table. The Sammy Whammy crowd was in a frenzy. Ludo raised his arm for a super slam. Sammy moved back to receive it. Ludo swung—deliberately missing the ball, then catching it with his paddle—and gently popped it over the net. Sammy couldn't get to the net in time.

The crowd groaned. Some of Sammy's fans pointed their fingers at him and hissed.

Ludo was overjoyed. He wanted to jump the net but instead jumped the table. He shook Sammy's hand. "Great game, Sammy!"

"You're pretty good yourself, kid," Sammy remarked like a real pro.

Then, arm in arm, the two players headed to the bar for a beer.

After that, Sylvan spent most of his time at the ping-pong table. First, he watched Ludo beating one passenger after another. Then, Ludo showed him a trick or two with his paddle.

One day they sat at the bar drinking. "How did you learn to play so well?" Sylvan asked.

"You think I play well?"

"You sure do. I thought ping-pong was a silly game before I met you. Now I think it's an art."

"You nailed it, Sylvan. It is an art. It's an art that's kept me sane. But I didn't always play well. I had to work hard for every serve and smash I know."

The waiter brought a pitcher of beer to the table. Ludo lifted it to his lips. When it was half empty, he put it down, wiped his mouth with his finger, and leaned back easily in his seat. Several passengers stopped to stare at him, then moved on their way.

"When I was eleven," Ludo related, "a friend in school, Johnny Campbell, taught me how to play. He came from a long line of ping-pong players. His grandfather was a champion. Every afternoon after school we would practice in his basement. Pretty soon I became the best player in my class—even better than Johnny. I won the silver ping-pong Award."

"I'll bet your parents were proud of you."

"Ha. Parents? My parents didn't even know about it. When I told them, it was the worst day of my life. It all started when my father said, 'What's that silly thing around your neck?' I held up the award and answered, 'It's the Silver ping-pong Award. I'm the best player in my class.'

"'You're what?' my father asked.

"'Ping-pong?' my mother said in a voice like a broken chime.

"'That's right.'

"I don't think I ever heard anything as loud as the silence that followed. Finally, after what seemed like an hour, I heard my own voice saying, 'I'm the best player in my class.'

"After that, my father didn't speak to me for months. My mother spent the time crying, laughing hysterically, or breaking dishes.

"But I was determined that nothing would stop me in my pursuit of ping-pong. When my father went out to conduct his orchestra, I practiced my serves on top of his Steinway grand; when my mother went shopping, I volleyed against the kitchen wall. I even bought a monkey, put him on a table, and slammed balls at him, always watching his eyes to study his reactions. It was a great way to practice eye contact."

Ludo drained the pitcher of beer. Then he ordered another.

"Talking makes me thirsty," he went on. "Especially when I talk about these lousy memories. Beer makes them easier to remember."

He gazed at the setting sun; a cool breeze blew across the deck.

"I went at ping-pong with a passion," he said. "I played after school, on weekends, on holidays. I read every book on ping-pong, went to every club, picked players' brains, competed with the best, studied, learned. I wanted to become the best!

"Too bad my love of the game wasn't shared by my parents. But, of course, they're not interested in dentistry, either."

"Maybe they're jealous of you," Sylvan suggested.

"Jealous of me? Ha. Why would they be jealous of me?"

Sylvan wondered why himself. Physically, Ludo was so ugly he made Schlossberger look like a movie star. His manners were bad, he had no charm, no money. . . . What was it that made him attractive?

"It's really strange, Ludo, but I feel jealous of you, too."

"I take that as a compliment. It's to your credit that you can admit it."

Sylvan fiddled with his beer glass, absently pushing it across the table. "Maybe it's because you have something I don't."

Ludo looked puzzled. "What is it?"

"I don't know; but, in spite of your miserable home life, you enjoy the things you're doing. For example, your enthusiasm for ping-pong has brought me into the game."

"It's a great game," Ludo said. "I've got a passion for it."

"*Passion.* You've got passion! That's what I'm jealous of. I wish I had it."

Ludo shrugged. "I can teach you how to play ping-pong, but I can't teach you how to have passion."

"Once I had it—but I lost it."

"You had it?"

Sylvan nodded. "In high school, in college, I practiced the violin all day. I dreamed about it. I lived for the violin. It was a great time in my life. What commitment! I only wish I could get some of it back now."

Ludo pondered Sylvan's words. "That wasn't commitment. That was compulsion."

"What do you mean by that?"

Ludo held up his hand. "Take it easy, Sylvan. All I'm saying was you were running away, hiding in your violin."

"But what about the passion I felt?"

"What you call 'passion,' I call disease. Most of it was probably rechanneled fear."

"Then what is passion?"

"A gift. It comes when you love something. It can lead you to mysterious, wonderful places. But once you start looking for it, you'll never find it. Passion sneaks up on you. All you have to do is be ready to accept the gift when it comes."

"I'll accept it. I only wish it would come."

Ludo refilled Sylvan's glass. "It'll come."

"I hope you're right."

"I am."

A loudspeaker announced that supper was being served. Sylvan finished his beer.

"I hope you're right," he repeated as they headed towards the dining room.

CHAPTER SIXTEEN

Bulgaria

I T`S GOOD TO BE back," Sylvan said as the *Ile de France* pulled into Le Havre. Ludo rubbed his hands. "Soon my work will begin. My train goes straight to Rome."

They watched dock workers pushing crates and moving baggage. It was a gray morning. Fog horns sounded in the distance. Sylvan put up his collar to protect himself from the chilling dampness. "I'll miss you, old friend," he said. "Give me your address."

Ludo pulled out his wallet and took out a business card. "Write me. I want to hear about your adventures." He zipped up his jacket. "What a greeting," he grumbled. "Fog's so thick I can't see a thing."

"Le Havre's a grimy town," Sylvan said. "The fact you can't see it is a good sign."

The line of passengers entered Customs, where they were herded into five separate lines. "*Ici, ici!*" shouted an agent.

After Customs, Sylvan extended his hand to Ludo. "It's time to part."

They shook hands firmly. Ludo picked up his valise and

pushed his way through an exit door. "See you in the States," he called back before disappearing down the stairs.

Sylvan boarded a train heading first to Paris, then to Vienna, Belgrade, and Sofia. On ship he had decided not to visit Madame Lefebre. That was too reminiscent of his old life. He wanted a new path, a new direction.

He passed sleeping berths and private compartments until he arrived at an empty car. Sliding across the straw seat, he placed himself by the window and gazed down an alley of shuttered windows and plantain trees.

During the three days it took to reach Belgrade, Sylvan amused himself by reading the signs as they changed from one language to another. He had no trouble with French, and figured out words in Italian and even German. But when they crossed the Yugoslav border, he found Serbo-Croatian quite complicated.

On the second night of his journey, he was joined in his cabin by a Serbian orthodox priest. The priest greeted him by saying, "Serbo-Croatian, French, same."

"You mean they're similar?" Sylvan asked.

"Same."

"Are you sure? I thought Serbo-Croatian was a Slavic language, and French a Romance language."

"Same," the priest repeated.

"I don't think so—but I'll look into it."

"Same."

Later, Sylvan learned that "same" was the only English word the priest knew. But he did smile a lot and kept offering Sylvan home-baked bread.

In Belgrade the train broke down. This forced our hero to change trains and be re-routed through Romania. Arriving in Bucharest early Monday morning, he took a bus to the Bulgarian border, worked his way through Customs, crossed the Danube, and finally arrived in the industrial town of Ruse.

Sylvan had not come to Bulgaria totally unprepared. In the United States he had purchased books on Bulgarian history, and more important, on the Bulgarian language. He had learned the Cyrillic alphabet pretty well, and also such basic phrases as: *"Dobro utro"*—good morning; *"Dobre den"*—good day; *"Leka nosht"*—good night; *"Dovizhdane"*—goodbye; *"Blagodarya"*— thank you; *"Molya"*—please; and finally, *"Da"*—yes, and *"Ne"*— no.

No one at the bus stop in Ruse spoke English. No one spoke French, German, Spanish, or even Russian languages of which Sylvan knew at least several words. He was suddenly forced to use his limited Bulgarian vocabulary. This, coupled with pantomime and gesture, were his only tools of communication.

He went to the ticket booth and said, "Ticket, *billeta, billet,* Sofia, Sofia." The man behind the window smiled. This was a good sign. But the man kept smiling no matter what Sylvan said, until Sylvan realized the man didn't understand what he was talking about. Some Bulgarians gathered around him. *"Engliski?"* one of them asked.

"Amerikanski," Sylvan answered. The Bulgarians became animated and chattered among themselves.

Sylvan held up his Romanian bus ticket stub: "Sofia, Sofia."

A squarish man with a broken tooth seemed to understand. *"Billeta,"* he said.

Sylvan nodded. *"Da,* yes, *billeta,* ticket—Sofia."

"Sofia." The man understood.

The other Bulgarians started saying, "Sofia." Then even the ticket seller knew. He smiled when Sylvan purchased his ticket.

The Bulgarians trailed Sylvan when he left the bus station.

From the curious way they eyed him, he sensed they had never seen an American before.

Two buses idled in a lot, black fumes pouring out of their exhaust pipes. Their drivers milled around, smoking cigarettes, talking, relaxing in the September sun. Sylvan approached them.

"Sofia?" he asked, pointing to one of the buses. Both men nodded.

At last, Sylvan had found the right bus. He tried his first Bulgarian thank you on the drivers, "*Blagodarya.*"

"*Molya,*" they answered.

Sylvan surveyed the other passengers on the bus. The women wore plain cotton dresses, the men 1930s Depression-style suits with white shirts and open collars. He took a window seat. His new Bulgarian "friends" had gathered outside. They waved to Sylvan, and called out "Sofia, Sofia." All were nodding their heads.

Sylvan got the message. He smiled, waved back, and felt reassured. He was on the right bus.

The driver took his seat at the wheel, revved up the engine, and started off.

The road straddled the Danube for several miles as it swept through the broken streets of Ruse. Aah, the Danube. Sylvan had heard about it since he was a child. Strauss' "Blue Danube" was his favorite waltz. In his idle moments, he often imagined a river of clear water reflecting the blue sky—a river created by God for stately vessels and elegant ladies. It is easy to imagine how disappointed he felt to find that the Danube was rusty brown with oil slicks, with fleets of Styrofoam cups floating down it.

Leaving Ruse, the road swung away from the river and crossed the Danubian Plain of North Bulgaria, passing through fields of corn, vineyards, and sunflowers—all products of the country's huge collective farms. The sun, blue sky, planted fields, and clusters of red-tiled roofs made it an ideal first day for a tourist.

They stopped briefly in Turnovo, medieval capital of the Second Bulgarian Empire, built like an impregnable fortress high on a mountain.

A big-boned peasant woman mounted the bus; a red kerchief framed her weather-beaten face. She had a big belly, large breasts, wide shoulders, and even wider hips. Stopping next to Sylvan, she tossed a sack of fruit on the rack above him, and sat down.

The bus pulled out of Turnovo. The woman rocked to the rhythm of the bus; her girth took up one-and-a-half seats; she chafed Sylvan's hips and crushed his shoulders. He tried forgetting his discomfort as they drove through the narrow streets of Gabrovo—humor capital of Bulgaria. But, the pain got worse. He must ask her to move over. But how? He knew so few Bulgarian words.

The bus went up a Balkan mountain road, passing historic towns where many leaders of the 19th-century revolt against Turkish domination had been born. When they rounded the legendary Shipka Pass, the peasant woman lurched to the right. Sylvan did not notice the magnificent view of the Thracian Plain spreading below him because his stomach felt like goulash.

He was about to protest when the road suddenly veered to the left, yanking his body in the opposite direction and throwing his head into the woman's lap. A gurgle of apology rose in his throat, but was immediately stifled by the two sharp turns in the road which threw him first against the window, then bounced him back against the woman.

At a loss for words, he said, *"Dobre den!"*

The bus swerved; again he slammed against her. His mouth

landed on her breast. A torrent of incomprehensible phrases followed. Sylvan hated to think what they meant.

"*Dobre den, dobre den,*" he panted through clenched teeth.

The road straightened; the bus stopped rocking. Things were improving.

Sylvan wanted to placate the woman. "*Dobre den,*" he repeated hopefully, his lips curling into a vapid smile. The woman, still steaming, stared stolidly ahead. Then she stood up, reached for her sack of fruit, and wielded it at her side like a mace. Sylvan knew that one false move, and he'd get the sack of fruit on his head. Stiffening, he fixed his eyes on the Valley of Roses, center of Bulgaria's perfume industry, and hoped she would forget about him.

She did. For the next two hours she snoozed at his side while he imitated the pose of an Egyptian mummy.

In the distance he saw tall buildings. It was a city. At last! The trip to Sofia had taken seven hours.

They passed a sign written in four languages. Sylvan came back to life. He read it. Sure enough, they were arriving in a city. But it wasn't Sofia—it was Plovdiv!

Plovdiv? Sylvan shook his head. Plovdiv? Where was Plovdiv?

He examined his map. Plovdiv was located in Central Thrace, about two hundred miles east of Sofia. "My God," he droned aloud, "how did I get here?"

It was too late to change buses or find a train. Might as well stay. Exploring Plovdiv—a city he had never heard of—might be exciting, he told himself. And hadn't that been the whole idea of the trip?

He followed the Bulgarian woman off the bus, walked a few blocks past a Byzantine church, past stuccoed walls of residential homes, and was soon standing in front of the Hotel Balkan. Mounting the marble stairs, he entered a lobby with a picture of Lenin and Todor Zhivko, President of Bulgaria, hanging on the wall.

Without a word, the clerk at the desk handed him a room key. He went up the steps to the second floor,and entered Room 225 with its view of a stuccoed wall across the street.

The trip had been exhausting. Sylvan decided to take a short nap before exploring the city. He hung his jacket on a hook and laid down. The springs creaked, the mattress sagged, but nothing could prevent him from falling asleep.

Three hours later he awoke refreshed. He looked at his watch. Only 3:00 p.m. He had lots of time to wash, take a shower, freshen up, and go for a walking tour of Plovdiv. In the bathroom, he discovered there was no bathtub. A drain in the center of the room provided the only outlet for the water. Evidently, the entire bathroom served as a bathtub. Sylvan had a good time brushing his teeth while he showered.

He put on fresh underwear, a clean corduroy shirt, well-pressed pants, and scentless socks; he combed his hair, polished his shoes, admired his face in the mirror, and marched out the door. He was ready for Plovdiv.

Would Plovdiv be ready for him?

He walked over to a kiosk and tried deciphering the Cyrillic letters on the magazines and newspapers mounted against the shelves. He spied a pamphlet in English: *Guide to Historic Plovdiv*. He decided to buy it.

He flipped through his English-Bulgarian dictionary to find the words for "How much?" but could only find the word for "How." He reached for the book, raised his eyebrows, and hoped the kiosk owner would understand.

The owner understood immediately. *"Cetiri stotinki,"* he said, holding up four fingers.

"Da," Sylvan answered, reaching into his pocket and pulling out a handful of coins. He wondered what they were worth. He held up the handful of coins while the owner shoveled through them.

"Cetiri." The man removed four coins and held them up for Sylvan to see.

"Dobre den," Sylvan said. He was getting pretty good at *"Dobre den."*

The pamphlet began:

> *Welcome to historic Plovdiv! Plovdiv is sec-*
> *ond-largest city in Bulgaria. We know you will*
> *enjoy this lovely city built on the wide banks of the*
> *Maritsa River—on a trade route that for centuries*
> *has tied up and down Asia with Europe.*
>
> *When Philip of Macedon conquered Thrace, he*
> *built the town and named it after the man he loved*
> *best—himself. Philip means "Horse Lover"; Plov-*
> *div means "Horse Loversville, " or, simply, "Philo-*
> *Polis. "*
>
> *When Thrace became part of Roman Empire,*
> *Philoppolis renamed Trimontium (Three Hill). At*
> *this time, the local population called Pulpudeva,*
> *which is Tracian translation of old Greek name:*
> *Philippo (Pulpu) and polis or city (Deva).*
>
> *After Slavs settled in Balkan Peninsula and*
> *town become part of Slav-Bulgarian State, it called*
> *by Slav name Pulpudin or Pludin. In 15th century,*

name of Poudin appears, from which present name Plovdiv, first mentioned in 16th century, is derived. After Turkish conquest, city is known as Phillibe, from 16th century onward.

So you see, dear reader, that etymologically and historically, city's present name is derived from Slav Pludin corresponding to Thracian Pulpudeva. Thus must the curious traveler admit to the varied but happy changes in city's name: Philoppolis, Trimontium, Pulpudeva, Pulpudin, Ploudin, Phillibe, Plovdiv. Indeed, the Thracian song writer, Racho Bistrovsky, whose famous song entitled, "Philoppolis to Trimontium to Pulpudeva to Pulpudin to Ploudin to Phillibe to Plovdiv and Back," is inspired by these historic changes.

Sylvan tried pronouncing the song title. He was so intent on getting it right, that he bumped into a lamppost and three pedestrians while "P-ing" his way along the sidewalk.

What a long history Plovdiv had! Why, Philip of Macedon himself might have stood exactly in the spot where Sylvan was now standing. Those dull history books he read at Westman were now coming alive. History was exciting if you stood where it happened.

He read on:

For further information of name changes and history, consult Paissii Hilendar's "Slav-Bulgarian History" (1762). Meanwhile, let us ask you, our reader, some questions.

You like history? You like sound of place names? Thrill of dates? Then call 254-7777, "His-

torical Help Line" for more facts of Bulgaria.

Send tax deductible contribution $35.00 to
"Historic Help Line," Garden City, Long Island,
U.S.A.

His explorations along the cobblestone streets of Plovdiv continued until he reached the Old Town. There, in a romantic and
peaceful setting, stood the magnificent houses of Baroque mer-
chants, with timber frames and lath-and-plaster walls. These
homes were now primarily occupied by Bulgarian artists who had
helped make Plovdiv one of the cultural centers of the country.

Sylvan meandered through the newly built Plaza, past shops
selling books, food, clothing, and paintings. He walked until the
sun set; electricity and starlight took over the city. At midnight he
returned to his hotel. Exhausted but exhilarated, he once more fell
into bed.

He awoke the next morning, grabbed a piece of brown Bulgarian bread from his suitcase, and charged down the Balkan Hotel
stairs. Any possibility of indigestion was smoothed over by the
lovely view of the Maritsa River outside his hotel. He strolled
along its banks. The water level was low. Men and boys stood
knee-deep, fishing. The wide promenades along the banks were
shaded with trees; polygonal pink bricks paved the long, straight
paths which were flanked by grass and wooden benches. In these
quiet, protected areas, lovers, philosophers, or tourists might rest
and gaze across the Maritsa through the black wrought-iron
fences, or, if they desired a more vigorous prospect, could turn their
heads to face the narrow street on the other side, with its traffic of
Muscovich cars, pedestrians, and bicycles. After living in New
York City, the pace of Plovdiv traffic felt peaceful and relaxing.
No one honked, and the drivers seemed very considerate of one

another. Later, Sylvan learned this was partly due to the strict Bulgarian traffic laws: One arrest for drunken-driving would cost you your license for six months; two arrests and you lost it for one year; three arrests, and you lost it for life!

It was Sunday morning. Families strolled along the promenade; the pace was slow and leisurely as they talked with one another.

Sylvan sat down on an empty bench and gazed into the Maritsa. Soon, a middle-aged man and woman sat down next to him. While they spoke in subdued tones, Sylvan thought he heard some English-sounding words. His ears perked up. Sure enough, sandwiched between Bulgarian sentences were such words as *slower, New York City, orange, Fifth Avenue, sewer,* and *park.* The clincher came when he heard the name *Macy's* pronounced with a thick Bulgarian accent.

Sylvan leaned towards the couple. "Macy's Department Store?" he said with a hopeful smile.

The man looked at his watch, then up and down the street. He mumbled something to the woman who was glaring at Sylvan.

"*Engliski?*" the man ventured hesitantly.

"*Amerikanski,*" Sylvan answered.

"*Amerikanski?*" The man looked puzzled. "*Amerikanski?*" he repeated. Somehow, the word "*Amerikanski*" had a soothing effect on this couple. They began to smile. "*Amerikanski, Amerikanski,*" they repeated.

"We thought you *Engliski,*" the man said. "We have bad enemy who *Engliski.*"

"Well, I'm *not* English."

They nodded.

"*Not* English!"

They smiled and kept nodding. The last time Sylvan had seen

nods like that, he had ended up in Plovdiv instead of Sofia. Baffled by the gesture, he decided to let the whole thing pass.

"Where did you learn English?"

"Oh, yes." The man twisted his mustache. "I learn America. I have been one year in New York City." He grinned, displaying a row of white and gold teeth.

"Did you like America?"

"Oh, yes. I like very much."

The woman agreed in a high voice. "He like very much."

Her red kerchief softened the bony features of her face, which, although middle-aged, had the wrinkles of a senior citizen. "I see you speak English, too," Sylvan said to her. "I like very much America," she answered.

"We are both there," the man said. He stood up. "Allow please to introduce myself. I am Penko, and this is wife, Lilyana."

Sylvan shook hands with them. "Glad to meet you. I'm Sylvan Woods. What is your second name?"

"That is Dardanovich," Penko answered. "We visit now Plovdiv, but we live in Sofia."

"Sofia? That's were I wanted to go."

"Sofia beautiful city. Sofia come from Greck word wise."

"Is that right?"

"It is right. People in Sofia very wise. That is how I go to America. I very wise. I spend whole year in New York sewers."

"Sewers? What were you doing in the sewers?"

"Is my profession," said Penko proudly.

"Did you like New York's sewers?"

"Oh, yes. I like sewers. I like America. I play music in America."

Sylvan straightened. "Music?" He knew the name Penko Dardanovich sounded familiar. Where had he heard it before? "What kind of music?" he asked.

"Good music—folk music."

"Did you ever play classical music?"

"*I love* folk music."

"I understand. But did you ever meet any classical musicians?"

"Oh, yes. I meet much classicals in New York."

Sylvan took a long shot. "Did you ever meet Sam Ferdinand? I played the violin, and Sam Ferdinand was my teacher."

"Good, you play violin," Penko said approvingly.

"But Sam Ferdinand, do you know him? He lives in New York too."

Penko wrinkled his eyebrows while he thought. "Ferrrdinand, Ferrrdinand," he said. "Sam . . .bushy mustache. . . much pick nose." Penko did a perfect imitation of Sam picking his nose.

"That's it!" Sylvan shouted. "That's him all right! By God, you do know him!"

"Ferrrdinand my best man. I like. I stay good his house two weeks."

Sylvan laughed happily. "I was going to look you up in Sofia. You saved me a lot of trouble."

"No trouble for me," Penko said.

"No trouble," Lilyana added, smiling and shaking her head from side to side.

Sylvan imitated her head movement. "What does this movement mean?" he asked.

"It mean, 'jes,' " Lilyana answered.

"What is jes?"

"Jes mean jes. In English you say no and jes."

"Oh, you mean *yes*."

"That right. Jes." Lilyana shook her head from side to side.

Sylvan shook his head the same way. "Jes, jes," he kept saying while visions of Bulgarians nodding at the Ruse bus station came to mind. "Now I know how I got to Plovdiv."

CHAPTER SEVENTEEN

Sylvan Learns to Folk Dance

A LTHOUGH PENKO AND LILYANA were both trained chemists working for the Ministry of Sanitation and Science, Penko's real passion was folk dancing—Bulgarian folk dancing. Lilyana liked folk dancing, too, and gladly accompanied her husband on his frequent trips into the mountains and villages to collect dances. This was, in fact, why they were in Plovdiv. It was the first stop of a two-week tour to collect authentic folk dance material to present at the Folk Dance Symposium in Sofia in November.

It occurred to Penko that Sylvan could be an asset to his research project. Not only could he and Lilyana have someone with whom they could practice English; but, more important, if he could interest Sylvan in folk dancing, and perhaps teach him how to dance Bulgarian style, he could prove to the cultural authorities in Sofia that Bulgarian folk dancing was an exportable commodity, a cultural product which could compete with the Soviet Union, Hungary, Yugoslavia, and other countries of the Communist bloc.

Penko and Lilyana conferred with each other. Then Penko

laid his hand on Sylvan's shoulder. "Sylvan," he asked, "would you join us in tour?"

"You mean travel *with you* in Bulgaria?"

Penko shook his head. "Jes, exactly right. I show you villages, teach you folk songs. I even teach you *how* to dance Bulgarski style. Then you go back to America; you teach other Americas and Sam real Bulgarski dances."

Sylvan was a student in his soul. He wanted to learn everything about Bulgaria, to enter the life of the Bulgarians and understand their country from the inside. What better opportunity than by traveling with a native—and a knowledgeable one at that?

"I'd like that very much," he answered, trying to restrain his excitement.

Penko beamed. "Good, very good."

"I happy for us," said Lilyana.

Penko took Sylvan by the arm. "Now we celebrate, eat lunch, drink." Together they marched towards the Stoyanov, a small restaurant with six tables and two surly waiters. Seating themselves by a window, Penko ordered a Shopska salad—lettuce, tomatoes, and grated cheese—and ample servings of grilled meats.

"When young man, I part of folk dance troupe in Sofia," Penko related while the waiter put the food before the three celebrants. "We make tour of Bulgaria, Romania, Hungary, and Poland. Soon I rise; I become head choreographer! I very proud! Lilyana join troupe and direct costumes." He signalled the waiter to bring more wine. Putting his arm around Lilyana, he whispered, "Quickly I love her. She love me. But strict rules in troupe; no fraternize with troupe members. Because of these rule, I choreograph my masterpiece!"

"A masterpiece?" Sylvan said, impressed. "I'd like to see it."

"I cannot show in small restaurant. Someday, maybe." He

sipped more wine, then began chewing a piece of veal. "What kind of dance was it?"

"Secret love dance."

Sylvan moved closer. "Tell me about it."

"I learn love code for dance," Penko explained. "My dance steps tap out message in love code. Only Penko and Lilyana understand message." A satisfied look crossed his face. He leaned back in his chair. "Soon we get married."

Sylvan bit into a piece of veal. "I'd sure like to learn that step."

"Tomorrow."

"You'll teach me that love step?"

"Tomorrow you learn other steps, good steps."

"Why? What's happening?"

"In morning we meet big Plovdiv choreographer, Kiril Kukudova." Penko rose from the table and flapped his arms like an eagle in flight.

"What kind of step is that?" Sylvan asked, trying to imitate it.

"That is Dobrujan dance from northeast Bulgaria. Tomorrow you see more.

That evening, after leaving his new Bulgarian friends, Sylvan went for another walking tour of Plovdiv. This time he almost raced down the cobblestone streets of the Old City.

What an adventure! A personal tour of Bulgaria led by native Bulgarians with a passion for folk dancing! He would be visiting villages no American ever heard of, seeing places Americans never dreamed existed, talking to the people he met. Penko and Lilyana were perfect interpreters; all he had to do was understand their English.

He knew so little about Bulgaria, it was hard to imagine what his adventures would be like. As he crossed a bridge spanning the Maritsa River, his fertile mind conjured up pictures of old, run-down villages, stout peasant women wearing red kerchiefs and colorful dress picking corn in the fields, fierce men with black mustaches thrashing wheat, breaking rocks, driving trucks, and grumbling to each other. He envisioned a gray stone building in the middle of a big city—Sofia, perhaps—housing Communist Party headquarters where somber men in black suits hurried through iron doors.

The pictures raced through his mind—then faded. Again, he realized he knew almost nothing about Bulgaria. It was hard to imagine where he would be going.

He decided to put his faith and trust in Penko and Lilyana. They were his guides—perhaps sent by a higher power; they would lead him through this strange, unknown land.

On the following morning, his guides drove him to the Hotel Traikisko, a twelve-story modern hotel with sculptures of World War II soldiers guarding its front entrance. Entering the marble lobby, they went down two flights of stairs before coming to the basement dance class. The rug had been rolled back, revealing a tile floor.

On the right, musicians in street clothes warmed up. Sylvan watched a heavy-set man put his arms through the straps of an accordion. A white-haired player—the eldest of the group—was blowing through a flute called *kaval;* it made a hollow, reedy sound. The Thracian seated to the left tapped lightly on his *tupan.* Chairs and tables had been pushed into a corner. Near the doorway, a thin musician sat on a stool; he held his three-stringed violin, the *gudulka,* between his legs and bowed it like a cello.

The white-haired man raised his *kaval* in an up-beat. Suddenly, the primitive wail of the Bulgarian bagpipe, the *gaida,* filled the room. Sylvan couldn't help comparing its mellow sound to the shrill Scottish bagpipes he'd heard at parades in the Bronx. Its haunting cry chilled his bones. He could easily imagine the Bulgarians suffering under five hundred years of Turkish rule.

Then, the plaintive gaida tune changed into the wildest of melodies. Sylvan was transfixed; goose pimples spread over his body. The orchestra was playing Bulgaria's most famous folk dance, *Pravo Horo*.

"Come, dance!" shouted Penko, pulling our hero by the arm.

"I'm really not a good dancer," Sylvan apologized. "I'll just watch for now."

Penko paid no attention to Sylvan's apology, but simply seized him by the hand and dragged him into line. "Dance!" he insisted. A powerful agricultural worker with a handlebar mustache and heavy boots grabbed his other hand, saying, "Asega."

Sylvan tried returning the greeting. "Dobre den, Asega." "Asega not name," said Penko. "Asega mean 'now.' *Now* we dance!"

"But I don't even know the steps," cried Sylvan, in one last attempt to escape.

"Steps not important." Penko raised his right foot. "Follow me!"

With Penko pulling him on the right, and the agricultural worker pushing him on the left, Sylvan had no choice. He began to dance.

He soon discovered that Penko was right. The steps were not important. There was no such thing as a "mistake." Glancing at the other dancers, he saw that many didn't know the steps either— or rather, they were doing different steps. Obviously, there were many variations to the Pravo; dancers used the ones they knew, or improvised new steps.

Sylvan began to get into the mood; his self-consciousness and awkwardness soon disappeared. Somehow, his feet moved in the right direction, even though he accidentally stepped on Penko's toe. Moving to the music, swaying with the line, he cried out, "Asega!" and "Heee-ho!"

When the music ended, everyone applauded. Sylvan smiled broadly. He applauded, too.

The next dance, *Trite Puti,* was so fast, Sylvan didn't have time to step on anyone's feet. Instead, he stumbled and flew with exhilarating speed, ending the dance with a victorious "Yahoo!"

The teacher turned to him, and clapping his hands twice, cried *"Bravo, Amerikanski!"*

Bucimis had a beat so complicated, Sylvan stepped on his own feet while dancing it. Yet the Bulgarians did it easily.

While Sylvan panted, Penko lifted his hand and explained proudly. "We like these *rrrrhythms.* We are born with them. We grow up with them." He slapped his thighs, tapped his knees, producing a complicated pattern of beats. "Here is seven beats in measure: One-two, one-two, one-two-three, one-two, one-two, one-two-three. Is *Ruchenitza* rhythm."

Sylvan tried beating it out. He slapped one leg, then the other, but the rhythm was so strange and different that he felt himself slipping, first into "Johnny Comes Marching Home," then into "The Star-Spangled Banner."

"Quick, quick, slow; quick, quick, slow," Penko explained again, slapping his legs harder. On the word "slow," he hit his right thigh. "After Pravo, Ruchenitza most famous dance in Bulgaria."

Sylvan tried again. By hitting his thigh until his hand turned red, he was finally able to get the *feel* of Ruchenitza but only in one leg. Tapping the other thigh did little good; but when he tried smashing it with his open palm, the Ruchenitza feeling quickly occurred. "I'm getting it," he panted. "Quick, quick, slow; quick, quick, slow. I feel it!"

Penko put his ear to Sylvan's leg and listened carefully. "Harder with right hand," he urged. Sylvan slapped away. "Better, better," Penko commented. "Hit more harder! Good, good." Penko straightened; his eyes glowed. "You have it. You have Ruchenitza!"

Sylvan beamed as he flagellated himself to the Ruchenitza beat.

Penko stood up. "In Sofia, we dance Ruchenitza in lines; we hold belts." Grabbing Sylvan's belt, he pulled his student out of his seat and nimbly danced a few lightning-quick Ruchenitza steps. "Hold my belt!" he ordered.

Penko's feet traveled rapidly across the floor as he continued lecturing. "In Sofia, Ruchenitza is line dance, but in other regions Bulgaria, Ruchenitza is solo, or sometimes dance with partner." He did a fast squat step. "Is improvised dance!" he exclaimed exuberantly, and, extending his leg, traced a circle by slapping his foot over and over again, as if gleefully exterminating cockroaches.

Taking their cue from Penko, the orchestra began playing a Ruchenitza. Sylvan could *see* it was improvised; all the Bulgarians started dancing a basic two-step in place. Some danced opposite each other; others hopped around chairs, stamped the floor, or faced the wall and shook their shoulders. One man flapped his arms, another undulated in the corner; a wraithlike woman pushed her palms forward, moving them up and down and around like a window washer; a scholarly student wearing rimless glasses snaked in and out of the door.

The teacher held up his hand. The orchestra stopped playing while he demonstrated three new variations: shoulder shimmy, neck rotation, and foot pedaling.

Sylvan tried them; they weren't hard. "Quick, quick, slow; quick, quick, slow," Penko puffed in his ear. "That is Ruchenitza beat."

Sylvan liked the *feel* of Ruchenitza so much that he kept dancing even after the orchestra stopped. While the teacher bowed to acknowledge the appreciative applause from his class, Sylvan was still dancing.

"You are good dancer," said Penko, pressing his arm around the convert and forcing him to stop.

"I like it!" Sylvan replied as the two of them walked to the door.

Several of the Bulgarians shook Sylvan's hand. They smiled, eagerly saying, "*Amerikanski, Amerikanski.*"

Sylvan nodded. Then realizing his mistake, he shook his head from side to side instead.

"*Da, da.*"

"*Amerikanski!*"

"*Da.*"

CHAPTER EIGHTEEN

The Wedding

THE NEXT DAY, PENKO, Lilyana, and Sylvan piled into their Muscovich and began their folk dance tour of Bulgaria. They stopped to buy some food in Asenovgrad, a town a few miles southeast of Plovdiv.

All at once, they heard music.

Lilyana's eyes brightened. "A wedding," she said. Sylvan was puzzled. "A wedding? But the music is so sad."

"Of course," Lilyana replied. "It is wedding." She called Penko from the food store. "Wedding music always sad," she said as they hurried towards the music. "Father loses daughter; mother loses son. Very sad."

"I thought weddings were a happy occasion."

"Later comes happy."

They looked down a cobblestone street for signs of the procession. The music grew louder. Wooden shutters flew open; women with red or black kerchiefs tied around their heads leaned out of the windows.

The musicians—led by a burly gaida player—rounded the corner. As the gaida wailed, a drummer, wearing baggy pants, slowly beat his drum with his hand; the drooping mustaches of the accordion and clarinet players gave their faces a mournful look.

Sylvan looked at the stony faces of the bride and groom. Both were impeccably dressed; the bride held a bouquet of red and white roses in front of her white bridal gown; the groom wore a black suit, white shirt and tie, and polished black shoes. He also carried roses, and a red handkerchief was pinned on his lapel.

Behind the bride and groom, family and friends followed, the men dressed in suits, the women in cotton dresses with colorful patterns. Many carried flowers, or had red or white handkerchiefs pinned to their lapels.

"We join them!" Penko said.

"Can we do that?" Sylvan asked. "It's not our wedding."

"Jes. Is custom."

The three of them walked with the others in silence. They passed through a plaza with stone sculptures in the center and a modern hotel to the right. Gypsy boys—the only poor people Sylvan had seen in Bulgaria—begged for *stotinkis*. Penko shooed them away with a few Bulgarian expletives.

The procession moved through a residential section. Asphalt streets, shops, new brick buildings. Bulgaria was rapidly changing from an agrarian to an industrial economy, and signs of building were everywhere. The country was growing and prosperous.

Soon the orchestra passed an iron gate and entered a court. On the right were tables and a dancing area; on the left, more tables, a restaurant with a kitchen in back, and pictures of beer bottles hanging on the walls. Straight ahead stood a platform for the musicians.

Neither pausing nor missing a note, the orchestra mounted the platform. Family, relatives, and friends moved closer. Silence.

The groom bowed to the bride; he handed her his bouquet.

She lowered her head, accepting them with modesty. Murmurs of approval. The bride gave her bouquet of roses to the groom. Family and friends craned their necks for a better view.

Bride and groom embraced. Everyone cheered. She smiled; he smiled, too. The somber mood lifted. Everyone laughed, shook hands, embraced one another. The orchestra struck up a lively dance in a major key.

Sylvan recognized the rhythm; he even recognized the tune—it was *Pravo Horo*.

A line formed, led by the bride's sister. Some dancers held hands; others leaned on neighboring shoulders; a few of the men grabbed belts.

Just then, the bride's father reached for Sylvan's hand and pulled him into the line. Another man grabbed his belt.

The line of dancers snaked around the courtyard. The music was hypnotic. After repeating the basic Pravo step he had learned in Plovdiv over and over again, Sylvan relaxed and shouted, "Hee-ho! Asega!" when the spirit moved him. So did the others.

A pebble got in his shoe. When he stepped on it, the pain was excruciating. "Yaaaiiii!" he cried.

The bride's father—a handsome, muscular man with jet black hair combed diagonally across his forehead—believing his American guest was shouting for joy, encouraged him by saying, *"Dai go zhivo!" (Give it Life!)*

"Yaaaiiii."

The man on Sylvan's left shook his head approvingly. *"Dai go zhivo,"* he panted.

The pain in Sylvan's foot got worse. Every time he stepped on the pebble, it felt like a spike driven into his heel. He wanted to leave the line, but as he tried wrenching himself free, the bride's father only tightened his grip and increased his shouts of encouragement.

Sylvan tried jumping, leaping—anything to take the weight off his heel. He hopped on one leg, spun on his toes, knocked his knees together, swung his heel high in the air. Tears streamed down his face. Thinking them tears of ecstasy, the Bulgarians spurred him on.

The music ended. He sat down on the cobblestones. The bride's father pulled him to his feet. Other dancers crowded around him.

"Bravo, bravo!" they shouted as they clapped their hands.

Penko's voice broke through the crowd. "Bravo, Amerikanski! I like Amerikanski dance style!"

Sylvan hobbled to a bench. He took off his shoe, held it upside down, and tapped the sole. A large pebble fell out. He took off his sock and looked at his heel. No blood—only a black-and-blue mark.

Relieved, he sat back to watch the Bulgarians pinning money on the bride's dress. Then, feeling better, he pulled an American dollar out of his pocket and hobbled over to her. "Dobre den," he said, pinning the dollar on a patch of empty space near her collar.

The bride lowered her head in acknowledgment of the gift, and fixed her eyes on Sylvan's foot. He had forgotten to put his shoe back on. She looked at him again, smiled strangely, and moved away.

"*Molya*," the bride's mother said, pouring Sylvan a shot of sliva. He raised the glass in the air, toasted "*Dobre den!*" to the bride, and felt his throat burn as he downed the sliva in one gulp.

Sylvan had many more shots of sliva as the afternoon wore on. The pain in his heel went away. He put his arms around Penko and Lilyana. "This is *fun*," he belched. "*Dobre den*. It's really fun!"

Downing another sliva, he joined the line for the next Pravo. A warm feeling of camaraderie swept over him. The festive atmosphere, the sliva, the music and dancing, the aroma of roasted veal and fresh vegetables, the smell of beer, the blue sky, the fresh air and sunshine, all combined to make it a special moment for him. Something was happening inside him—something strange, but familiar. Still, he couldn't quite make out the odd feeling coming over him.

Found

CHAPTER NINETEEN

Return

THE DANCE ENDED. THE groom's father offered Sylvan more sliva. Sylvan raised the glass high in the air and, declaring, *"Molya,"* downed it in one gulp. Then he began chattering with the people around him. Never having met an American before, they bombarded him with questions, none of which he understood. But lack of comprehension did not prevent him from answering. Deftly wielding his six-word Bulgarian vocabulary, he modulated his voice and added pantomime, grimaces, gestures, frowns, smiles—and two more glasses of sliva—with such skill that he managed to express himself on every subject of importance from the architecture of Thomas Jefferson's mansion in Monticello, Virginia, to the proper proportions of meat and breading used in the preparation of American frankfurters. On top of this, he piled exhortations for universal brotherhood and through an elaborate battery of facial movements, told the story of his childhood in the Bronx. He even pantomimed a description of the Museum of Modern Art.

Each time he answered a question with an unrelated answer, his Bulgarian hosts agreed with him by shaking their heads side to side and offering him more sliva.

Then the orchestra played Ruchenitza. No partners necessary; no lines needed. Ruchenitza was a free-form dance. Sylvan remembered the basic step, complete with Penko's timing instructions: quick, quick, slow; quick, quick, slow.

Amidst cries of "Ruchenitza!" many who had not danced the previous Pravo Horo rose from their tables. A man dressed in a khaki army suit and combat boots began stamping his feet wildly on the stone floor, accidentally crushing a wine glass. "Hi, ho, heee!" he cried.

A swarthy man with black hair and huge eyebrows took off his jacket and rolled up his sleeves. "Brr!" he roared, shaking his shoulders and rotating his arms like two windmills. Two young girls did a window-washer movement with their hands; another girl's necklace flashed as she performed pirouettes in front of her partner—a fatherly figure whose white hair flew in all directions as he rhythmically slapped himself on his thighs, chest, arms, and hips.

Near the door by the beer keg, two men on their knees clapped out Ruchenitza rhythms, oblivious to the open spout and the puddle of beer forming in front of them. A grandmother did two-steps and shoulder shakes opposite her granddaughter who flailed the air with her arms, imitating a crow in flight. Even a man with a broken leg stood up, and supported on his crutches, tapped his good foot and blinked to the music: Quick, quick, slow; quick, quick, slow.

"Dance, dance!" Penko encouraged.

But Sylvan didn't need encouragement. "Dance with *me!*" he cried, grabbing Penko by the hand and waltzing him around the courtyard.

"No, no," Penko pushed him away. "Is no waltz. Is Ruchenitza! When you dance Ruchenitza, you *feel your soul!*"

So saying, Penko pulled Lilyana out of her chair and began dancing opposite her with flirting eyes and flying feet.

Sylvan imitated Penko's two-step. Then, as he got more comfortable with the music, he started making up his own steps. At first, they were but variations of Penko's two-step. But he expanded it to a three-step, adding shakes and arm rotations.

Had *he* done that? Sylvan Woods, the man who couldn't even dance a few days before, now choreographing his own steps! He smiled in satisfaction.

The Ruchenitza modulated to a new key. Volume increased; rhythm got faster. A surge of enthusiasm swept through the dancers, bringing shouts of "Ho, ha!" and "Hi, ya!"

Sylvan was carried away by the enthusiasm. His improvisations became faster, wilder.

Flashing eyes, shaking shoulders, flying feet—Sylvan's world was whirling. The dancers, waiters, tables, chairs, bride and groom-even the orchestra grew distant.

Again, that strange yet familiar feeling.... When had he felt it before? The wind of inspiration rushed through him; he felt in touch with a greater spirit.

He forgot who he was.

He forgot where he was.

He forgot why he was.

He was having an *attack!*

He sprang into the air; he knocked his knees together and sang strange tunes.

The other dancers moved out of his way as he took up more and more of the dancing area. His toes rat-tat-tapped on the wooden portion of the floor, while his neck stretched back and forth like a cobra.

At last, the Ruchenitza ended. But Sylvan kept dancing! The

Bulgarians formed a circle around him, clapping, shouting, and urging him on.

Sylvan leaped high in the air and came crashing to the ground. "Ooh," groaned the Bulgarians. Some rushed to aid him, but he jumped up, whirled away from them, and pirouetted over the cobblestones. Then he did a cartwheel towards the kitchen, where he grabbed the chef's high white hat, clamped it on his head, and started pantomiming a stew, throwing imaginary meatballs not only into a cauldron, but all around the courtyard, as well. Then, kicking the pot with his foot, he began slapping out Ruchenitza rhythms—quick, quick, slow; quick, quick, slow—on his face, thighs, and chest.

He ended his performance with Russian squat steps which left him folded on the floor. But he jumped up, he bowed, blinked his eyes, and walked off the dance floor.

The Bulgarians cheered.

"Amazing!" Penko said, leading his pupil by the arm to a chair. "What you do?"

"An attack."

"Attack?" Penko looked bewildered. "What means 'attack'?"

"Hard to explain. I feel better. . . . I feel whole again."

Penko examined Sylvan's face. He took his pulse. " 'Attack'? 'Whole again'? What this means?"

Although Sylvan didn't quite understand it himself, he tried explaining to Penko. He tried for the next hour while the wedding ended and Bulgarians departed.

"It's my meeting with God."

"God?"

"I tune in to my unconscious processes."

"Eh?"

Lilyana joined them as they walked back to their car. "I am

reacquainting myself with my creative center. . . ."

"What means 'reacquainting'?"

They drove through the darkened streets of Asenovgrad while Sylvan used English, Bulgarian, French, and some pantomime trying to explain.

"Jes," said Penko finally.

They drove in silence. Finally, passing the town of Dospat, north of the Greek border, Sylvan declared: "I'm going to put my life together."

"Good idea," Penko observed, steering the car around a boulder that had fallen on the road. "You fall apart dancing Ruchenitza; you need put self together."

"I need a place where I can be alone to think."

"You must think," Lilyana said. "You have trouble times."

There was another long silence. The Muscovich puffed its way up the winding mountain road.

"I have it!" Penko exclaimed.

"What?"

"You fall apart dancing, jes?"

"Yes."

"You want place to put self together, jes?"

"A quiet place. . . . Yes."

"Rila Monastery."

Lilyana shook her head from side-to-side in agreement. "Where's Rila Monastery?" Sylvan asked.

"Pirin Mountains. We pass on way to Sofia."

"Sounds like what I need, a retreat."

"Is very good," Penko said. "You reacquainting yourself. In monastery, many people go to reacquainting."

"Yes. *Yes.* That would be just what I need."

CHAPTER TWENTY

Monasticism Revisited

T HE NEXT DAY, AFTER driving up a steep road flanked by towering mountains, they arrived at Rila Monastery. Penko parked in the lot behind a Balkantour bus. Sylvan stepped out, took a deep breath of fresh mountain air, then surveyed the maze-work of stone and timber rooms rising behind the wooden gates.

The monastery had been built during the Middle Ages at the foot of Mount Musala—the highest mountain in the Balkans. The jagged incline of its rock, its wild, unapproachable summit, its snow-covered fringes, seemed a worthy enough symbol of God. Sylvan could imagine medieval monks cringing in the shadows of such a fearsome deity.

Lilyana leaned out of the car window. "I sad you leave us."

"I am, too," Sylvan said, "But I must have time alone to think."

"Thinking good," Penko added, tapping his forehead with his finger. "I sad, too." He stuck his hand out the window.

"We shake hands. You visit us in Sofia, jes?"

"I'll try to. But I really can't promise anything right now. I need to be alone."

"Young man must to think," Penko remarked philosophically. He rolled up his window, waved goodbye, and backed the Muscovich out of the parking lot.

"*Dovijdane,*" Lilyana called as the car rounded a curve and disappeared from view.

Sylvan took another deep breath of mountain air. He held it for a long moment, then exhaled slowly. It tasted salubrious, invigorating. You don't find such air in cities, he thought. Gods and mountains must work together. He wended his way up the cobblestone path, passed beneath the wooden gate, and entered the monastery.

Cobblestones paved the courtyard in front of him. Straight ahead stood a basilica with scenes from Christ's life painted in frescoes on wooden panels. Although the number of monks had diminished since the Communist takeover, their quarters were still intact, preserved by government interest in the history of Bulgaria, and by a few faithful priests—mostly old—who marched across the courtyard ministering to the needs of the monastery. The first floor was given over to rooms for study, meditation, or prayer, and to kitchens, refectories, a library, and a museum, recently completed, which contained objects and artifacts from the monastery's long history.

An old monk approached. His beard, long white hair, and black cassock dress made him look like the original patriarch of the Bulgarian Orthodox Church. Strangely, he seemed to know exactly what Sylvan wanted. He took him by the arm and led him silently across the courtyard, past fountains, where Sylvan stopped for a drink of delicious mountain water, and up the stairs to the monks' cells on the second floor. Their shoes echoed down the corridor until they arrived at a door on the west side of the monastery. The monk turned the iron knob, pushed it open, and bade Sylvan enter.

The room was simple: a bed, a desk, a chair, and a window overlooking a mountain stream below.

It was all he needed. The old monk made Sylvan understand that meals were served three times a day in the common hall, and since Sylvan could hardly speak Bulgarian, he would be assured of little or no conversation.

"*Molya*," he thanked the monk. The old man answered with a soft Bulgarian sentence of which Sylvan understood nothing. Then he left, the clumping of his heavy shoes fading as he disappeared down the corridor. An absolute silence descended.

Sylvan entered his room, closed the door, sat down on his bed. He listened. His breath stopped.

Silence.

The silence rang in his ears. What a beautiful sound! Paradoxically, it seemed to be the loudest sound in the world. Silence soothed him.

Now he understood why pilgrims went on retreat, why wise men went to the mountains. They wanted to meditate; they wanted to recapture the dream they had lost in the wild world below.

Sylvan wanted to meditate; he wanted to recapture his dream.

He waited for the silence to speak to him.

During the weeks that followed, Sylvan slowed down. He meditated in bed, strolled through the corridors and courtyard, and tried weaving the threads of his life together. He kept a journal to record daily events. Sometimes he wrote in it just for therapy. His journal was a place to "think out loud" and express anything he wanted without worrying about what others might say. Whenever he wrote in it, he went on a journey of self-discovery; and on this journey, he hoped to find the *real* Sylvan Woods.

He wrote:

> *Where am I? Good question. I'm in a no-man's land, a half-way house. I'm waiting for a direction.*
>
> *I'd like a creative direction. It's romantic, but uncertain. Lots of ups and downs, highs and lows; it's a roller-coaster life.*
>
> *I like riding the roller coaster.*

Wherever he went, he carried the journal under his arm; it began to feel like part of his body. After meals, while monks mopped the kitchen, swept the floor, and cleared the dishes, he sat at the refectory table and wrote.

One morning as he sat in the basilica, facing the carved golden cross, his eyes wandered over the stone sculptures of saints and angels and fixed on the frescoes of biblical figures painted on the walls. He watched the rays of sunlight stream through the stained glass window and closed his eyes in meditation. Surrounded by heavenly silence and beautiful art, he wondered if there might be a connection between the energy and joy he felt during his attacks and the power of God. The Bulgarian Orthodox Church had built this basilica to help Bulgarians worship God. It was a public place where members could have their own kind of private attack. Perhaps there wasn't much difference, he ventured, between this public church and the private church inside him where his attacks took place.

Sylvan rose and walked around the courtyard; he liked walking around the courtyard.

He liked hiking in the mountains even better. There, among the trees and rocks, by the brook, he felt mysteriously alive. The mountain breeze cooled his face, and when he looked up at the wild snow-capped peak of Mount Musala, marveling at the deity that created it, he yielded to the power of the Nature around him.

Later that day, when he lay down on the grass, he took out his journal:

> Mendelssohn was my favorite composer. Beethoven was Dr. Lume's favorite. Mendelssohn and Beethoven—two free spirits.

That afternoon, after supper, on the way back to his room, Sylvan walked through the refectory kitchen. He had never seen such a kitchen before. Huge cauldrons filled with soup sat on a gigantic greasy stove; hundreds of pots hung helter-skelter on the walls. There were slabs of meat hanging from hooks, vats of milk, caves with wines and wheels of cheese, sacks of beans, peas, potatoes, and cans of spices. There were tomatoes—hundreds of tomatoes— piled in baskets, strewn over counter-tops, lined up on shelves, and stuffed into half-open closets. Sylvan remembered seeing them on the table at every meal—even breakfast.

He picked one up the size of a grapefruit and ran his fingers over its soft curves. Thousands of years ago, during pagan times, when primitive tribes worshiped sun, moon, river, trees, and vegetation goddesses, perhaps they also worshiped tomatoes. He remembered reading Plato's *Republic* at Westman. Looking at the tomato, he philosophized about its nature. Was this tomato a reflection of the *Idea* of Tomato, the perfect or *Heavenly Tomato?*

As he considered this, he thought he heard the tomato talking to him. He glanced around the refectory. Was anyone watching? Monks? Priests? Luckily not. Maybe they were busy listening to their own tomatoes.

Sylvan fixed his eyes on the tomato: Eyes popped out of its skin; a nose squeezed through; bushy eyebrows sprouted ... familiar bushy eyebrows. A mouth formed, and a voice came out of the mouth, a familiar voice—the voice of . . . *Sam Ferdinand!*

The first words were unclear, resembling some primitive language. But, soon Sylvan understood; he heard the word intoned: "Violin!"

The tomato almost fell out of his hands. In a flash, his decision was made. A new direction! Return to America—to the *violin!*

He thought about his lessons with Sam. He never felt lost and alone playing the violin. Violin had been his gateway to attacks, to improvisations, and to the mysteries of creation.

Yes, it was time to open the violin case, time to improvise and compose music, time to return to America.

Time to go home.

Sylvan's revelation came as a shock. He had come so far—and for what? To complete a circle? To come home to the violin?

He decided to take a walk; he went down the stairs, passed through the arched doorways, and crossed the courtyard. A July sun fell on the cobblestones under the cloudless sky; stones of the basilica shone under its brilliance; pine trees blanketed the surrounding mountains, and the smell of resin filled the air. A priest stood in front of the basilica. When he saw Sylvan, he walked over and handed him a letter.

"Molya," Sylvan said. He examined the letter: United States stamps, Roman letters, familiar handwriting. A letter from his mother. He sat down at the edge of the fountain to read it.

> *Dear Sylvan,*
>
> *Hello, my darling boy! We miss you. The house is so quiet. No music. No phone calls. The post of-*

fice even misplaced your letters, so we haven't received any.

Sylvan, July 12th is coming—that special day. Sam came by last week and said, "Why should we miss his birthday just because he's not here?" He proposed that we celebrate your birthday in Bulgaria! Then he phoned Gussman and Schlossberger; they're coming too! I don't know how he did it; but you know Sam.

We're flying to Sofia on July 11th. Then we'll come to the monastery. We're all very excited.

Love,
Mom and Dad

Sylvan couldn't understand it. How had they tracked him down? He hadn't written home for weeks. Maybe Sam had been in touch with Penko. Still, how had he gotten Schlossberger to come? And Gussman?

He walked across the courtyard. Mentally, he started rearranging his room, planning his reception. His legs slowed, speeded up, stopped, moved on, mirroring the movements of his mind. His past was coming to see him—people, it seemed, from another life. How would he deal with them? They were visiting him on his turf, Bulgaria, where he had rediscovered his vision.

That was it! He'd tell them about it, the return of his attacks, his decision to go back to music; he'd tell them about the changes he had made, and about the changes he was going to make. And his own metamorphosis— he'd trace it from the beginning. Sam, Gussman, Ma, Pa, Schlossberger they'd want to hear all about it. The conversations with Ludo, passion rediscovered, the mysterious workings of Ludo's inner life and his expression of it through ping-pong; the confusing Bulgarian nods which had landed him in Plovdiv rather than Sofia—had they actually been "plants" by some higher power (predestination, perhaps), ways of preparing his mind to meet Penko and Lilyana? He visualized an audience of Sam, Gussman, his mother and father, sitting around him, avidly listening to the stories of his adventures—his folk dance tour of Bulgarian villages, learning to dance Pravo and Ruchenitza, and finally, after a ten-year hiatus, *improvising* again. He'd tell them about Bulgarian dance music, history, geography, give them tips on language.

He puffed up his chest. For the first time in years, the future looked bright.

His erratic movements around the courtyard disconcerted the monks. He walked in circles, diagonals, straight lines, then suddenly zig-zagged to the right, only to shift into pensive backward walking; he headed towards the fountain, dashed back to his original position, then moved sideways towards the refectory door. A new thought was forcing him to move so curiously. How would he explain the return of his old behavior—his attacks—to his mother? In the past, mere mention of attacks would make her hysterical; she'd moan about how hard she had worked for her only son, and now this. She just didn't understand him. She understood the practical, "real life" problems as she called them—the hassles of daily existence. She was an expert on those. It was strange. Even with her insistence on such bothersome necessities as cleanliness, dress, food, she was the one who wanted violin lessons for him. She found Sam, found money to pay him, and insisted that her son take lessons. She had tolerated baseball, basketball, and whatever, but music she had adored. Music was her alter of worship. Other professions were okay—tolerable, but basically they existed merely to make a living. But the arts, ah, the arts, and especially, music! Artists created something out of nothing. They performed magic. She could never understand how they did it, but the mystery of it galvanized her. Yes, she worshiped it.

Sylvan was surprised. He had never thought about his mother in these terms. In the past, he had seen her mainly as an over-whelming *presence,* someone who guided and controlled his life, either through her own efforts, or through the efforts of "hired hands"—mostly teachers. In the beginning, he had even felt that way about Sam. But Sam won him over; and Sam's teaching was fantastic.... Still, he had never stepped back and taken a good look at his mother. He had never seen her other than as a mother. What kind of human being was she?

Sylvan stopped in his tracks. A human being? His mother? What a startling thought! It had never occurred to him that she might have her own life, an existence apart from him. Why not? Separation at that early, violin-forming stage would have been un-thinkable. But now he was twenty-six years old. Separation was definitely thinkable. In fact, as Dr. Lume had said, it was imper-ative. Even Schlossberger had hinted at it when he sold the Gilded Mines stock to her. Sam, too, in France, had had that funny look in his eyes, conveying the thought that Sylvan's views and the *weltanschaung* of Mrs. Woods were substantially different.

What was the difference? Finding it would reveal a key to Syl-van's personality.

He pictured himself ten years old, practicing the violin in his room, dreaming of notes flying in great swirls of messianic music, notes inundating his room with heavenly sound, creating Michae-langelo patterns of color on the ceiling of his Bronx Sistine chapel. Then he'd lie on his bed and dream about the God of Music.

That was the difference! Dreams! In the past, his mother had stood in direct opposition to his dreams—or so it seemed. She had opposed their expression by opposing the directionless, formless, chaotic burst of energy in his attacks. Maybe his attacks assaulted her sense of control, both of him and of herself. It was scary losing control.

Sylvan understood this fear. He often felt it just before an attack. Sometimes he gave in to his fear. In the past few years he had given in to it constantly, with the result that nothing was created, and he had remained stagnant, depressed, and dead inside. But how wonderful when he had worked with his fear, worked with the energy it engendered, then transformed that energy into a unique moment of creation! That was an *attack!* The joy he felt afterwards was beyond expression. He would remember these moments for weeks; no, years. In fact, as he walked in the courtyard, he remembered with pristine clarity every attack he had ever had. He realized these were the moments he lived for, the visible and dramatic peaks of the mountain tops; they made his life a worthwhile, memorable adventure.

Dreams were the difference. Could his mother ever understand his dreams? Could he explain them? Maybe they were beyond her ken, even beyond his ability to explain. Maybe they just frightened her too much. But he wanted to tell her, wanted her to understand him. He vowed to try. After all, he wasn't a kid anymore. It was time to stand up for himself, to fight, to explain himself to others. And his mother was the ultimate other.

He drew back, surprised at the thoughts he was thinking. Was this an epiphany? He felt himself separating from her, and his vision growing.

What of his father? Where did he fit in? What would he tell him?

He saw no trouble telling his father anything. Pop seemed to accept whatever came his way. He never judged his son. Sam and his father were similar in one respect. They accepted his dreams and his attacks. Sam had always told his mother that dreams are an important part of art. His father never said this, but he hadn't denied it, either. Often, Sam verbalized what his father might have said if he were more verbal. In any case, telling Sam and his father would be easy; they'd be a good audience.

Sylvan paced, oblivious to the stares of the monks and priests, unaffected by the hot rays of the July sun, or the splashing fountain and its gentle echoes across the monastery courtyard. He wondered again about the source of his inspirations. No doubt this source was locked up in every human being. A secret power. Pristine vision. Everyman's link to the Cosmic Mendelssohn. But it was a link most chose not to recognize.

Sylvan wondered why.

Memories returned: Gussman conducting, waving his arms in disbelief while Sylvan switched from Mendelssohn to Beethoven, to Bach, Mozart, Lalo, and finally dancing and improvising wildly; his mother, sobbing in the audience; his father's casual acceptance; Sam's enthusiastic shouts of "Bravo!"

Why didn't his mother, father, even a musician like Gussman, acknowledge this curious power? Would access to it drive them to the edge of madness—divine madness? When Sylvan improvised, it often felt like he was going mad. His mother agreed. She'd knock on his bedroom door whenever the wild improvised tones came out of his violin, and bring him vegetables, sandwiches, cakes—anything to make him stop. Gussman disapproved of it, too. Only Sam supported him, and with some reservations, Sylvan sensed. Perhaps secretly, they all wished they could dance, sing, and shout with joy as what Sam called the Lord of Music swept through their being. Screams of the soul, a tornado, a chaotic, formless madness breaking boundaries with the frightening possibility of driving the unprepared recipient to the asylum. No, you cannot be unprepared; you cannot stand helplessly before the terrifying power of such divine Madness. Rather, Sylvan realized, you must *prepare yourself* for it. That was it! Another answer. He would tell his mother and father, Sam, Gussman, everybody! Preparation for Madness was his goal. He'd strengthen his body, train his mind, return to the discipline of music. And through music, he would develop the power to *receive the Madness* and transmute it into art.

Years of searching had come to an end. The primal vision could be restored, and expressed on a higher level. He would make his attacks work for him, molding the latent energy into a visible presence: the living, dancing, shimmering joy of mad dancing shoes.

He passed the refectory door and rounded the basilica. Suddenly, he heard a girl's voice cry, "Sylvan!" He turned. Long black hair, Roman sandals. Sylvan caught his breath.

"Linda!" Sylvan squeezed her in his arms.

"Didn't you get my letter?" she asked, rubbing his bony shoulder.

"Linda, Linda, what are you doing here! Wow, who'd have guessed." He kissed her again. "Letter? What letter?"

"I sent you a letter."

"I never got it. Where did you send it?"

"Hotel Vitosha in Sofia. I mailed it out about a month ago." Linda looked dismayed. "I'm really disappointed. It was such a good letter, too."

"I never got to Sofia," Sylvan explained. "I took the wrong bus, and ended up in Plovdiv."

"I didn't have any problems like that; I came straight from Salonika. Too bad you didn't get my letter."

She pointed to the edge of the fountain. "It's a long story. Let's sit down."

A group of monks near the refectory door were staring at them. Not many women came to Rila.

"When I finished graduate school at Westman," she went on, "my parents gave me a present: a trip to Greece. I started off by visiting relatives in Salonika. Then I went to Athens, Corinth, and Delphi. After three weeks of traveling, I decided to write you a letter. When I finished, I figured, well, Bulgaria isn't far, why not visit you there?"

"I'm glad you came," he said, touching her hand. "How did you find me?"

"By accident. Your mother gave me your Hotel Vitosha address in Sofia; but when I asked about you, they never heard of you. I knew something was wrong. I was disappointed, but decided to make the best of it. I traveled around Sofia, took side trips to Koprivshtitsa, Bistrica, Kjustendil, and a village called Gjusevo, where I saw a fantastic dance called Ruchenitza. Ever heard of it?"

Sylvan smiled knowingly. "I've heard of it."

"A bus driver in Gjusevo told me about Rila Monastery, about the healthy Bulgarian mountain air, and peaceful surroundings. I figured I'd visit. It's exciting. I've never been to a monastery before."

"It's really different," Sylvan said. "Come, I'll show you around."

They got up, crossed the courtyard, and went into the basilica. Icons stared at them from the walls. Silence. "This is my favorite spot," Sylvan whispered. "I'm not religious, and Jews don't go to basilicas anyway, but being here makes me feel serene, peaceful, even religious. I like sitting in this pew and sewing my life together."

"How's the sewing?" Linda asked.

"I've made a breakthrough."

"Really?"

"I've found peace."

"Aren't you too young to have found peace?"

"What I mean, Linda, is I'm not as wild as I used to be. I see both sides. I'm more measured."

"And how about your attacks? Don't you miss them?"

"I've discovered dancing."

"You? Ha, that's a laugh. You're such a klutz."

"Not anymore. Oh, I'm not graceful like you, but when I dance, I feel like my old self again. Folk dancing. I've learned folk dancing—Bulgarian folk dancing."

"I've seen those dances. They're pretty wild."

"It's true," Sylvan agreed. "I danced at a wedding two weeks ago. Since then, I've been feeling great. I've been thinking about these forces in my life—you know, the inspirational energy that invades me when I have an attack. I've been thinking about inspiration versus self-control and discipline; how to combine them and use my energy creatively, and not just fall apart."

"You mean fall apart like in the Mendelssohn?"

"Right. Since Westman, I've been trying to keep myself in check. The result has been misery and depression. But since I danced at the wedding, I realized my goal is to combine inspiration and discipline." Sylvan paused thoughtfully. "I'm beginning to understand that inspiration plus order equals perfection."

Linda listened, surprised. Sylvan had never spoken like this.

"Very wise," she finally said. "You've matured."

Sylvan agreed. "It'll make my parents happy when they get here."

"Your parents?"

"Tomorrow's my birthday," he said, taking the letter out of his pocket and handing it to her.

"My God, the whole crew's coming!" she gasped, handing the letter back to Sylvan.

Sylvan returned the letter to his pocket. "Let's keep this tour going," he said, rising from the pew. "You haven't seen my room yet."

"Haven't we been through this before?"

"Not in Bulgaria."

They left the basilica and recrossed the courtyard. When they passed the fountain, Sylvan noticed a short, hooded priest in a black robe with a rope tied around his waist. As they walked up the stairs to the second floor, the priest followed them.

Sylvan couldn't imagine why they were being followed—if, indeed, that was the case. He opened the door to his cell, led Linda in, and closed it behind him. He heard the priest walking by. His footsteps stopped at an adjacent cell door which opened and clicked shut. Sylvan forgot about him.

"It's a simple room; but it fills my needs."

"I like simple things."

They sat down on the bed. Sylvan put his arm around her. "It's peaceful in here," he said. "You can meditate or just be alone with yourself. I guess that's why Ivan Rilsky chose this area in the first place.

Linda moved closer to him. "Who's he?" she asked softly.

"Ivan Rilsky—St. John of Rila—he was a Bulgarian monk."

Linda moved closer still; her eyes looked directly into his. "Does he still live here?"

"Are you kidding? He started this monastery in the 10th century."

"That was a long time ago," she whispered, pressing her warm cheek against his.

"Yes," he gulped. "But Rilsky didn't have a cell like this to meditate in. For years, he led a holy life living in trees and caves, until he finally chose this spot in the Rila Mountains as a permanent place for his devotions."

"It's good to meditate," Linda breathed.

They lay back on the bed. Linda's shoes fell on the floor.

"His piety brought him great fame," Sylvan continued. His shoes fell on the floor. "Soon people knew he possessed unusual powers; he could exorcise demons and cure diseases of the body. Four times a year, devout pilgrims came to the monastery, sometimes as many as 15,000. Before the communists took over, Rila Monastery was the center of the Bulgarian religion, kind of what St. Michael in Normandy was to the French."

"I l-love the French," Linda stammered. "They have moats around their monasteries."

"Around their castles," were Sylvan's final words.

It had been many years since those days in college when Sylvan and Linda had gloried in one another's company. Together, now, somehow they felt the same as in their early days together, their best days. They hadn't recaptured the spirit; the spirit had recaptured them.

Sylvan cradled Linda's head against his shoulder as she slept in his arms. Our hero heard Ivan Rilsky's staff pounding on the floor, welcoming him to the monastery. Sylvan smiled inwardly; he closed his eyes and dozed in blissful sleep.

But, even as he slept, he kept hearing Ivan Rilsky's staff pounding on the floor. Then he heard it knocking on the walls—even the ceiling. Ivan was knocking everywhere.

Linda looked up. "What's going on around here?"

"I don't know." Sylvan sat up. The banging on the wall stopped—then started again.

Linda lifted her head. "Is that your neighbor?" she asked.

"I never knew I had a neighbor."

The banging started again. This time it was so strong, bits of plaster began falling from the ceiling. Sylvan jumped out of bed. "This is ridiculous!" he snapped, as a white cloud of powder rose from the floor. He threw on his pants. "I'm going next door. Who does that guy think he is, anyway?"

He stormed out of his cell and pounded on his neighbor's door. A shuffle of feet. The door opened. A short, hooded priest stood in the doorway. Sylvan was about to grab the towel hanging around his neck when he spied the word *Bloomingdale's* stamped on its label.

Again he looked at the priest's face: the round, cherubic face of a man in his mid-forties, a face with thin lips and pin-ball eyes which darted back and forth in their sockets like laboratory mice trapped in a cage. . . .

"My God!"

"Am I your God?" Dr. Lume inquired.

"How. . . . Where. . . . What are you doing here?"

Lume's eyes kept darting. He looked Sylvan up and down. Sylvan took his arm. "Come into my room and sit down. No. Let's go into your room."

"Let us stand here," Dr. Lume suggested. "We will become better people if we stand on our own feet."

"Of course, of course. I forgot about that. Well, this is turning into the craziest day." Sylvan tapped his cheek in bewilderment. "But why are you here?"

Dr. Lume looked Sylvan straight in the eye; he twirled his waist-rope. "Why are *you* here?"

"I came to find myself."

"And?"

"I'm making progress."

"Progress?"

"Progress."

"Progress."

"Yes, I'm making progress."

Dr. Lume tilted his head. "Progress, progress," he repeated several times to himself.

"Dr. Lume," Sylvan asked again, "I still don't know why *you're* here."

The doctor thought a moment. "Neither do I."

"You don't?"

"No."

"Then why did you come?"

Lume stroked his chin. "A good question. I thought that by coming, I could find out the reasons for my coming. But upon reflection, I believe it has something to do with my wife leaving me."

"I never knew you had a wife."

"Well, she left me, anyway." Lume squeezed the edge of his robe with a steady relentless rhythm.

"It caused an imbalance in my life. I went to more Beethoven concerts after that, and saw God more often. We became good friends. Finally, one day, He said 'Why don't you visit me?' 'Where do you live?' I asked. 'In Bulgaria,' He answered. So I took the first plane over. When I landed in Sofia, I asked a policeman where God lived, and he gave me this address." Lume took a folded piece of paper out of his pocket and opened it. *Rila Monastery*, it read in Latin and Cyrillic letters.

"Do you like it here?" Sylvan asked.

"Oh, yes, it's very peaceful. I've always needed religion, but in America I was too busy working. It's nice to try it with a friend, especially if that friend is—you know who." Lume glanced up at the sky.

"And how is your violin playing?"

"Ah, the violin." Lume raised his head; a far-away look filled his eyes. "I gave it up."

"What! After all the work I put in on you!"

"I have no need for it anymore."

"What about your practicing—and your concert in that public school?"

"The concert was a great success, or at least, I thought so. I had a standing ovation in the middle. Then I realized the audience was walking out." Lume looked sadly at his hands. "Short fingers, you know. They always do you in."

"That's terrible. You must have been really embarrassed. How humiliating—to have the audience walk out on you."

"Yes, it was sad. Only Yonkle and Sadie remained. But, of course, she is a paraplegic; and Yonkle takes care of her. They had to wait for the aide." Lume shook his head. "I did feel low for awhile; that is, until I went to a Beethoven concert. Then, every-thing was alright. Beethoven always cures."

"What did Beethoven say this time?"

"He said, 'You don't need instruments to play my music; you only need a mind, and an inner ear to hear it.' I realized I have all that. Why torture myself playing the violin? When I left the con-cert, Beethoven and I took the subway home together. Then, as we had Danish and coffee at Dizzy's Diner, he told me to stop wasting my time giving therapy, and that I would cure more people—in-cluding myself—if I went to a quiet place somewhere and thought about music."

"It's certainly quiet here," Sylvan said, glancing through the window at the ridges of richly forested mountains and rocky sum-mits surrounding the monastery.

Lume looked through Sylvan's half-open door. "It *was* quiet." We disturbed you?"

"You didn't disturb me; you disturbed the music. You disturbed Beethoven!"

"Beethoven can take it. He's a strong composer." Lume grew pensive. "Yes," he agreed. "That is why he gives succor."

"He sure succored you. Remember that concert at Carnegie? You were wild, Dr. Lume. I've given that concert a lot of thought, and I think you overreacted."

"Never!" Lume exploded indignantly. "One cannot overreact to Beethoven. He is the ultimate psychotherapist."

Sylvan's tone softened. "I mean instead of going wild and waving your arms and tossing and turning to the music, sometimes it's better to just sit still. Let the music fill your mind; let it swirl in your brain and wash every cell. I think it's a question of *learning* how to listen. If you don't hold it in your mind, the music loses some of its power."

Lume's eyes started to glow. "Power," he groaned, "yes, I'd like power. It makes my hands feel bigger."

"Makes you feel bigger, too," Sylvan added.

"Where did you get so smart?" Lume snapped.

"What do you mean?"

"You're speaking differently. There's been a change. You're not the same as you were in my office. Your ego has shifted a notch upwards." Lume looked pleased. "All that therapy finally worked."

"It's true. I feel differently about myself. I was really lost when I came to you; I'd lost rhythm; I'd lost music; I'd lost the sense of who I am."

Lume stroked his chin. "Acute symptoms of Beethoven-Loss," he summarized.

"Mendelssohn-Loss, to be exact."

"Mendelssohn, Beethoven, it doesn't matter. They're all the same."

"Yes. Well, music has come back to me."

Lume relaxed his face; his eyes stopped darting. "Tell me about it."

"My attacks have returned. I get them through dancing—folk dancing."

"Dancing is good. Many of my patients dance. It is one of the great forms of play."

"I think so," Sylvan agreed. "It's like combining Mendelssohn and basketball."

"Precisely."

There was shuffling behind Sylvan as Linda came to the door. She had slipped on her dungarees and buttoned her shirt. "Who is this creep?" she asked.

"This is no creep, Linda. This is my shrink, Dr. Lume."

"You mean *him?*"

"Sort of," Sylvan answered, putting a protective arm around Dr. Lume. "He taught me many things, too."

Linda offered her hand. "Glad to know you."

Lume took her hand; but, rather than shake it, he examined it carefully, palm up. "A beautiful hand," he muttered, and turned it over. "Such long fingers," he added wistfully.

A gong sounded. "That's the lunch bell," Sylvan said to Linda. "The food here is simple but good."

"I like simple things," she repeated.

Lume licked his lips. "I can't wait for those tomatoes." Lume's last words were accompanied by the backfiring of a car. Sylvan looked out of the window. A gray Muscovich had driven into the courtyard, followed by a green one. "They're here!" he shouted, grabbing his wash-and-wear shirt and slipping it on. "Let's go!" He dashed down the hall, buttoning his shirt as he ran. Linda followed close behind, while Lume trailed in the background mumbling something about seraphic intercession. Sylvan went down the stairway three steps at a time, and burst through the doorway in time to see his father stepping out of the gray Muscovich. Then came his mother, and Vladimir Gussman wearing dark glasses. As Sylvan raced towards them, he saw Sam Ferdinand's bushy eyebrows through the front door window.

Penko and Lilyana were stepping out of the green Muscovich when Mrs. Woods spotted her son. "Sylvan, Sylvan! There's my boy!" Tears were streaming down her face. "Sylvan, darling," she cried, throwing her arms around his neck.

His father embraced him, then looked him up and down. "You're leaner, more muscular. And I like that mustache," he said.

"It must be the Bulgarian food," his mother cut in. She squeezed the muscle in Sylvan's right arm.

"No, Ma, it's the dancing."

"Dancing?"

Penko scurried over. "You glad we bring friends, jes?"

"*Da*, Penko. And such a mob."

"Mob?" Penko asked. "What means 'mob'?"

Sam approached, wearing his pin-striped suit. Sylvan grabbed his teacher's hand and shook it vigorously.

"I called Penko before putting this trip together," Sam explained.

"Your idea, eh, Sam? Of course. I knew you'd figure something out. You always do."

"If not for Sam," Mrs. Woods broke in, "you would be celebrating your birthday alone."

"That's right," added Sylvan's father. "If not for Sam, we'd probably still be in the kitchen eating meatballs."

Sylvan's father hugged him again; so did his mother.

Sylvan playfully pushed them away. "Hey, hey, I'm glad you came, but I'm getting mauled by all this love."

His mother backed off. "Sylvan is right. All this attention is tiring; he needs rest." She turned to her husband. "Harry, get the lunch out of the car."

"I'm not hungry now, Ma. But you eat something. Meanwhile, I'll tell you about what's happening to me."

"We all want to hear," his mother said, "but let's eat first." Harry handed her a bag filled with sandwiches, fruit, cakes, napkins, and two thermoses. She passed the food around.

Sam declined her offer. "I'll eat later," he said, leaning towards Mrs. Woods. "I think this is a good time for Sylvan and me to have that talk," he whispered.

"Oh, yes," she whispered back. "Now is the time." She turned towards the other members of the party, and pointed towards the fountain. "Let's sit over there. We can eat in sun while Sam and Sylvan go for a walk."

Sam and Sylvan crossed the cobblestones and headed toward the Byzantine arch.

"I'm glad we can be alone," Sylvan said. "There's so much to tell you."

Sam loosened his tie and opened the top button of his shirt as they left the monastery. A steep descent took them down a ravine to an open field strewn with boulders; to their right, a brook cascaded over flat rocks; in the distance stood the sunlit peak of Mount Musala.

"What's changed?" They walked along the brook. "I see notes in your eyes," Sam said. "There's no sign of stocks or therapy in them—"

"You see that?"

"Of course. It's obvious to anyone, especially your old violin teacher who knows you so well. I see lots of things but I select only a few to tell you. A teacher never tells his students everything he knows. No. Timing is always of the utmost importance. Students have to be *ready* to hear you."

Sylvan was impressed. He had always respected Sam. Now he was seeing another side of him. They headed towards Mount Musala; trees carved playful shadows out of the brilliant sunlight.

"When a crack appears in their wall, I jump in with a piece of advice," Sam went on. "If my timing is right, it works. Then they get an idea, and voila, it's the same idea I've planted in their minds a short time ago. Only it comes out *their* way."

"You don't see stocks or therapy in my eyes?" Sylvan asked. "What does that mean?"

"It means that Schlossberger and Lume are no longer part of your future; or, if they are, they'll take new forms. Before you went to Herman, you needed something different. You'd been in school too long; you needed a break—a mental rest. You needed to put music to sleep for awhile. Working on Wall Street was perfect. You learned about the world of finance, supported yourself, saw life beyond music. I'm sure Herman will agree. We talked on the flight from New York. He even remembered his violin lessons with me, and spoke fondly about them."

"What about therapy?" Sylvan asked, thoughtfully. "You said you didn't see that in my eyes, either."

"Right. I've never met this Dr. Lume, but I'm sure he has been important to you. After Westman, you needed time to pull back, analyze your past, your motives, your direction. It's all part of the growing-up process. But I doubt you'll be needing therapy—at least for now. You've resolved many of your conflicts. The lost years are ending. You're ready to go back to your real work."

"My real work?"

Sam nodded. "I'm sure you know what that is."

"Music."

"That's where your heart is. Everything else is okay; but for you, it's peripheral, a hobby, footnotes to the main text."

"Sam, you're terrific! You read my mind. That's exactly what I was going to tell you. I want to go back home; I want to play the violin again, take lessons, see if I can make a life in music.

"I sensed that."

"You're the only person who knows, now—you, and Linda."

"Linda knows this?"

"She's the first one I told; you're the first one who's guessed."

"Linda's a smart girl. Maybe she'll be part of your new direction."

"I hope so."

They sat down on a rock overlooking the meadow. A few puffs of white clouds dotted the sky.

"And your attacks?" Sam asked.

"They've returned; but through folk dancing, Bulgarian folk dancing. It happened at a wedding. I started dancing, and then it hit me—an attack, like old times."

"Like the Mendelssohn."

Sylvan nodded as he remembered back. "I got carried away. I never knew I could dance like that! What passion, what power! I loved it. I want to do it again and again."

"I'm glad to hear that. You've found your personal spark plug." A long moment of silence. Sam sat pensively on the rock. Finally, he said, "You know, Sylvan, I used to have attacks like you."

"Really?" Sylvan was startled. "You! A teacher! You had attacks?"

"Yes. But in those days, we didn't call them attacks. It was called 'poetic inspiration,' or sometimes 'divine madness.' But whatever words I used, the feelings were the same. How do you think I could understand you so well if I hadn't gone through it myself?"

Sylvan was stunned.

"I still have these moments of poetic inspiration today," Sam continued, "only not as many. I'm too involved in my music school and administrative details. My mind is too occupied with worldly pursuits to have them too often. Still, even in my busy life, they come periodically; and I'm glad for that. They're my personal visits from the Lord of Music."

"Wow! Sam, do you have some idea of my future?"

"No one has that, Sylvan. Not even Schlossberger, as you've no doubt found out. Oh, I have a vague idea of the future; but it's so vague, it wouldn't help you much. No, the future is like the present—more of the same voyage of self-discovery."

"That is pretty vague. Still, I'm interested."

"Well, there are two parts to the living adventure," Sam explained. "First is finding the spark, the inspiration. The second part is, once you've found it, what do you do with it." He paused meaningfully. Sylvan waited. "The answer is, you spend the rest of your life trying to give it away."

"Give it away? What do you mean?"

"The spark is of such a nature, Sylvan, that if you don't give it away, it dies. That's because this spark, inspiration, divine madness, attacks, or whatever you want to call this cosmic force, is flow. It's energy on the move. That's why it's so important, once you find it, to give it away, share it, communicate it. That way, it stays alive in you and in others. That's why I decided to become a teacher. It puts me in a good position to give my sparks away. But, of course, you can do it in any field, as an accountant, performer, teacher, janitor, whatever. The type of work doesn't matter. Only the thoughts behind it do."

"You think that's my destiny?" Sylvan asked.

Sam shrugged. "I can't predict that, Sylvan. But it is something to think about."

They rose from their rock and walked slowly across the meadow. Sylvan thought about it in silence for a long time. "Maybe," he mumbled to himself as they passed trees, campers, and rocks. "Maybe," he mumbled to no one in particular as they headed back to the monastery.

Sam broke the silence by changing the subject. "My music school is flourishing. I'm getting lots of students. I've even hired a cello and clarinet teacher."

"That's good," Sylvan said wistfully. "I haven't taken a lesson for such a long time, I've almost forgotten what it feels like."

"Forgetting is good; it clears your mind."

"I like the way you put that, Sam."

"So do I. I'm glad you're coming back to the fiddle. You'll be a good advertisement for my music school. I hope my Bulgarian boys get some of your attacks."

"Bulgarian boys?"

Sam reached into his pocket and pulled out a black ledger book. "Here's my recruitment schedule," he said, opening the book to page one. "I've already signed up three."

Sylvan turned the page. Vergiliy Atanassov, Raiko Dimitrov, and Boris Karlov were listed in alphabetical order. "You're combining business with pleasure again, Sam. Just like France."

"I always do. It's a pleasure seeing you and a pleasure doing business. And, speaking of business, now that you've decided to start fiddling again, how are you going to support yourself?"

"I'll get some kind of job. Maybe Schlossberger will rehire me."

"Ask him when we get back."

"But I didn't see him. Where is he?"

"Not everyone fit into the car, so Herman and Ludo took another one."

Sylvan quickened his pace. "Let's hurry. Maybe they've arrived by now."

Sam glanced at his watch. "You're right. We've been out over an hour." He brushed the dust off his pants and walked faster. "Time to go."

They crossed the field and headed up the ravine. When they arrived at the monastery, a Muscovich was pulling into the courtyard and screeching to a halt. The front door burst open. Schlossberger rolled out, waving his arms. "Woods! Woods!" he cried, throwing his account books back in the car. "We had a tough time tracking you down."

Sylvan shook the broker's porcine hand. "You're one of my birthday presents, Herman."

"You bet I am!" Schlossberger's jowls flapped as he chewed his words. "I wanted to give it to you personally."

Linda, who was standing near the Muscovich, edged forward. "Give him what?" she asked.

Schlossberger turned. "Who's she?"

"Linda's a friend from college," Sylvan explained.

"Huh," he grunted.

"Well, what is it?" Sylvan prodded.

"A check!"

"Check? Check for what?"

Schlossberger broke into a broad grin. "Kid, remember that

Monarch Oil lease?"

Sylvan tried remembering. It had taken place so long ago—in another life. Yes, vaguely. I recall—"

"That lease was purchased by Oil-A-Can Company of Oklahoma. They drilled, and the well came in. Kid, you struck oil!"

Sylvan was dumbfounded.

"I wanted to give you your one-and-only check for the proceeds," Schlossberger rolled on.

The wheeling and dealing of the stock market came back to Sylvan. "Why only one check?" he asked suspiciously.

"Because," Schlossberger explained, puffing out his chest proudly, "I was smart enough to sell the lease for you at the right time. That was the only lease Oil-A-Can ever drilled successfully. Everything else they did failed. They went bankrupt a month ago. But I sold out long before that, put the money in your name. And here it is!"

Schlossberger handed Sylvan an envelope covered with gold stars. Sylvan tore it open. Staring him in the face was a check for $17,032.

"My God!" he gasped.

Schlossberger glowed. "I thought you'd say that."

"What a friend!"

"Take it easy, kid, take it easy. I didn't come to Bulgaria just to give you a check. I'm here on business. I'm negotiating a silver mining contract with the Bulgarian government." Schlossberger chuckled softly. "Maybe some day I'll corner the silver market."

Just then, Dr. Lume scampered through the refectory door. He was about to mingle with the priests when Schlossberger spied him. Shaking his head in disbelief, he roared out, "Lume!" He rushed over and threw his arms around the doctor.

"Get your disgusting hands off me!" Dr. Lume squealed. He

pushed Schlossberger away and brushed off his garments. "Can't you see I'm busy now? You must wait for an appointment, like everyone else."

"Dr. Lume, Dr. Lume!" Schlossberger radiated happiness. "I am so glad to see you. I've missed your services terribly. When are you coming back to America?"

"Tomorrow, next week, next year," Lume answered disdainfully. "Maybe never."

Schlossberger hardened. "Well, if that's the case, I'm staying here for awhile. I need a few sessions. It's been a tough year.

"I no longer practice," Dr. Lume replied, raising his eyebrows.

"Just being near you will cure me," Schlossberger answered.

Dr. Lume hesitated. Then the tired look of the seasoned analyst crept back into his eyes. "Oh, all right, just this once." Schlossberger sighed with relief.

Lume's voice filled the courtyard. "Lie down. Ree-lax."

Schlossberger lay down on the cobblestones, while the Bulgarians looked on with amazement at what they took for a unique American religious ritual.

"Relax. Relax *more*."

Schlossberger stretched out flat on his back. Lume stuck a stray cobblestone under his head for a pillow.

"Are you relaxed?"

"I am, I am."

"Now, tell me—what is troubling you?"

"It's my wife, Doctor."

The Bulgarians strained to hear Schlossberger, even though they couldn't understand a word of English. The monastery courtyard—in an uproar only a few minutes before—became deathly quiet. Only the animalistic grunts and staccato phrases issuing from Schlossberger's half-dry mouth could be heard.

"Aah, which one is that?" Lume asked. "Eleanor?"

"No, Sarah."

"Aah, yes. Number 3."

"She's leaving me."

Lume twirled his waist-rope and looked bored. "This happens every three months."

"Yeah," Schlossberger groaned. "Whenever the market goes down."

"The market is down?"

"Yeah. Dropped over three hundred points. Yesterday, it went down another thirty."

Lume stiffened. "What about my Exxon—and my Federal Chicken?" he asked in a clipped voice.

"Everything's down."

Lume stamped his foot. "You fool, why didn't you sell?"

Schlossberger cringed. "You didn't call me." Then his face started turning red. "*You never* call me, never." He sat up, glaring at Lume. "Why don't you call me? I always call you. You don't care; you just don't care."

"Why didn't you sell, you fool? With a broker like you, I'll be broke soon. What do you think is supporting me here? Dividends! Yes, dividends—and capital gains, too. You can't become a monk on a shrink's pay. No, you need dividends." Lume raised his hands to the sky, beseeching that God he knew so well. "Dividends!" he cried.

Schlossberger smelled a crisis. He jumped to his feet. "Now, take it easy, Dr. Lume. It's okay. Don't worry. They'll come back. Exxon, Federal Chicken, the market; it won't go down forever. It's just a small correction."

"How much has Exxon 'corrected'?"

"It's trading at twenty-four now."

"Twenty-four! But I bought it at fifty!"

"It'll come back—and so will Federal."

"Federal's down, too?" Lume whined.

Schlossberger giggled oddly. "Seven."

"Seven? I bought it at thirty-two!"

"It'll come back, too. Look, the whole market is down. If oils have been smashed, what can you expect of chickens?" Lume wheezed, shaking his head.

"Things are bad in the States," Schlossberger continued. "Economy's down. I came here to get some business for the firm—"

"That's why your wife left you," Lume hissed.

"She'll come back, too," Schlossberger insisted. "Just like the market, she'll come back. It's just a correction." Slowly, Lume recovered his professional calm and sat down at the edge of the fountain. "Tell me about it," he said. "Things got bad when she started selling short," Schlossberger moaned.

"I know what it's like to be short," Lume mused, glancing down at his fingers.

"We had a fight. She kicked me out of the house. I had to move into my office."

"Did you sleep well there?"

"Yeah."

"You slept with your stocks."

"Yeah."

"Your stocks caressed you; they were loving and kind."

Schlossberger's eyes moved upward in his head, inwardly viewing the celestial movements of graphs, charts, price earnings ratios, and stocks. As he concentrated on this financial planetary show, his heaving muscles slowly relaxed. The magic of concentration was working.

"Your stocks love you," the doctor continued. "The money you make from them is more love."

"Hmm," Schlossberger sank back down on the cobblestones. He moaned beatifically.

"Tell me about them, Herman."

Schlossberger's eyes shut tight. He concentrated. Slowly, a vision worthy of Michaelangelo formed in his mind. "Yeah, I see 'em. They're hanging just under the Dow Jones average. Huge stocks, big companies, heavy feeders. . . ."

"What do they look like?"

"Round. Heavy. White. With nipples."

"Nipples?"

"Yeah, beautiful stocks." Schlossberger's hands reached upwards as if to hold one of his stocks. He kissed a balance sheet, sucked an imaginary dividend; his jaws closed gently on some long term debt, he sucked earnings.

"You love your stocks."

"I do, I do."

Lume leaned down. He whispered in the broker's ear. "Speak to me, Herman. Tell me about *Her*."

"Yeah, yeah," was all Schlossberger could say. For the next fifteen minutes, he gazed dreamily at the firmament of his inner financial heaven.

Soon, he felt better. He sat up, yawned, stretched.

A Bulgarian priest walked over. He offered Schlossberger a bed in Dr. Lume's room, an offering instantly vetoed by the good doctor, who screamed in protest, saying he wanted nothing to do with this former mental patient. Instead, Schlossberger got a room next to his therapist—a cramped cell just large enough to hold a single bed. Here, surrounded by peace and quiet, the broker planned his big silver deal coming up in Sofia. He spent most of the night tapping out messages on Lume's wall and whispering between the floorboards.

Meanwhile, Ludo had just awakened from his nap in the back seat of the Muscovich. He squeezed out of the back door, rose to his full seven feet, and stretched while the Bulgarian priests gawked. How did that monster fit into the tiny back seat, they wondered.

When Sylvan saw him, he called out, "Got your paddles?"

Ludo tapped the breast pocket of his jacket. "Right here." He pulled out a ping-pong ball and twirled it at the end of his fingers. "Where can we play?"

"The refectory table," Sylvan proposed. "The monks will love it. They've never seen ping-pong played the way you play it."

"*We* play it," Ludo put his arm around Sylvan's shoulders.

"Hey, old buddy, great to see you. How was that dental clinic in Rome?"

Ludo's eyes lit up. "I'm telling you, Sylvan, the work being done in Europe is fantastic. So many new ideas, experiments, papers. And the best paper was given by a Bulgarian scholar, Sadi Momchik, on the 'Teeth of Bulgarian Saints.' Momchik claims that Bulgarian saints had the strongest teeth, and that if I wanted to learn more about them, I should go to Rila Monastery."

"Why Rila?"

"Evidently, the monastery has catacombs with skeletons of monks, priests, ascetics, hermits, and other men of God. Momchik told me to look at their teeth and see for myself. Of course, I don't care about monks' teeth, or priests' teeth, or even hermits' teeth. I want saints' teeth."

"Where do you find saints' teeth?"

"On saints."

Sylvan pondered a moment. "Maybe you ought to start by looking in the monastery museum," he suggested. "They've got old parchments, pieces of cassock cloth, medieval bibles in beautiful calligraphy, letters, crosses, suits of armor. Maybe they've got some teeth."

"Yes, that's it!" Ludo's eyes jumped wildly in their sockets. He grabbed a pile of dental books and his briefcase from the back seat of the Muscovich. Then he turned to his father who stood nearby talking to Sam. "Pop, I'm going to the museum to look for teeth."

"You talk to your father?" Sylvan asked with surprise. "Sure."

"I thought you hated your father."

"Sure. But we had a reconciliation."

"I'm glad. But how?"

Ludo grinned. "I started running."

"But you hate exercise."

Ludo leaned his elbow on the roof of the Muscovich. "True," he agreed. "But one day in Rome I was late and had to chase a bus for five blocks. When I caught the bus, I was panting. Then a strange thing happened; this weird peace came over me. I attributed it to the running. Breathing in all that air makes you feel good. I checked it out with some dentists at the conference, and they agreed. Anyway, it felt so good that the next day I decided to run around my hotel. Same good feeling. That was a month ago. I've been running every day; it's becoming a habit."

"What does all this have to do with your father?" Sylvan asked.

"Pop and I have something going between us," Ludo explained. He signalled his father as he started running in place. "Come on, Pop. Let's go!" Ludo ran across the courtyard. Gussman turned, dropped his conversation with Sam, took a deep breath, and charged after his son. Although the conductor was only five foot three, his spindly legs carried him across the courtyard with such speed that he soon caught up with his son. They raced past the basilica; neck and neck, they rounded the fountain; Ludo pulled ahead in front of the refectory door, but Gussman dashed past him. Sam and Penko cheered the conductor on while Sylvan and his father rooted for Ludo.

Suddenly, Gussman reached up and grabbed Ludo by the collar. Ludo stumbled on a cobblestone. Father and son fell on top of each other by the fountain. Ludo splashed water in his father's face; his father splashed back. They laughed and trotted back to their cheering fans, arm in arm.

Proudly, Gussman pointed to his son. "Piano is a good runner.

"My name is Ludo, Pop."

"Ludo Piano, fine runner," Gussman added.

Ludo turned to Sylvan. "My father still can't remember my name; but I don't mind anymore."

"Ludo, just speaking to each other is a victory." Sylvan faced Gussman, who was wiping his forehead with a handkerchief. "You sure can run fast, Mr. Gussman."

"Fast?" Gussman shook his head. "I just play with my boy." He patted Sylvan on the shoulder. "How is Mendelssohn?"

"I left Mendelssohn, Mr. Gussman. But I dance."

Gussman pulled a baton out of his vest pocket. "When I conduct Bulgarian People's Chorus next Friday, we have dance performance, too."

"You're conducting here? How did you arrange that?" Gussman pulled a silver baton out of his pocket, then a gold one. "I collect batons. I come to see Lushko Keremidchiev who has wonderful baton collection. He get me to conduct chorus."

"I'd like a job like that to pay my way back to America."

"Oh, Sylvan!" Mrs. Woods rushed over. "You're right. It's

time to come back."

"Funny, Ma. I came to the same conclusion."

"Really?" His mother's eyes were radiant.

"Yes," Sylvan said. "Hey, I've got a great idea. Let's celebrate my birthday, your arrival, and my departure. Let's have a party!"

"Party good idea," Penko agreed. "Come, we go to eat—room where is dance floor. We have good party." He opened the trunk of his car and pulled out a gaida.

"What's that?" Mr. Woods asked.

"It's a Bulgarian bagpipe, Dad. Penko's a great musician."

Penko filled the bag with air, put the chanter in his mouth, and began playing a Bulgarian folk song. He strolled towards the dining room; the others followed, hypnotized by the tune. Even Schlossberger, whose only previous experience with music had been the violin lessons he'd forgotten with Sam, and the sound of the ticker tape, was fascinated by the sound.

"He's an excellent player," Sylvan whispered to Linda. "I get chills whenever I hear the gaida. If it weren't for that music and the marvelous Bulgarian folk dances that go with it, I would never have had another attack."

"Attack?" Mrs. Woods looked stunned. "Oh, no! Sylvan! You didn't have another one of those."

"Indeed, I did."

Mrs. Woods started crying. "We spent so much money, sent you to so many doctors, sent you to college. . . ." She wrung her hands. "Why us? Why us?" she moaned. "Fate is so cruel."

"Mom, take it easy." Sylvan put his arm around her. "It's because of these attacks that I'm coming back to America."

Mrs. Woods brightened. "What do you mean?"

"Those attacks are my salvation."

"What do you mean, 'salvation'?" Mr. Woods asked. He

tapped his head. "Have you lost some screws upstairs?"

"No, Pop, not at all. In fact, I've found some of the missing screws. My attacks are the best things that ever happened to me; they're creative outbursts; they're communications with God; they're—"

"I know about God," Dr. Lume sighed. "He and Beethoven work together."

Mrs. Woods stopped crying. "You mean it's not a sickness?"

"It can be a very healthy thing," Sam offered.

"They're a lot of fun, too," Sylvan added.

"Fun?" Vladimir Gussman cut in. "You call forgetting the Mendelssohn Concerto fun?"

"It's improvising," Sylvan explained. "It's making up things on the spot."

"*Sounds* like fun," said Ludo. "Why don't you teach us how to have one?"

"*Da,*" Penko squeezed his gaida. "Teach, teach."

Ludo extended his arms above the throng: "We'll all have an attack *together!*"

CHAPTER TWENTY-ONE

Mad Shoes

PENKO TOOK SYLVAN BY the arm. "Teach!" he cried. "I'd like to, but I don't know if I can." Sylvan looked around at the expectant faces; even the monks and priests seated at the tables seemed eager to learn.

"Try," Sam encouraged.

Sylvan paced the floor. "Well . . . okay. The best way to teach it is—by dancing! Hey, Penko, play your gaida. Everybody up! We're going to dance!"

"I can't dance," Ludo protested.

"Sure you can, Ludo." Sylvan pulled him forward. "Anybody can dance."

His mother giggled. "I feel silly dancing—"

"Stand up, Ma."

Mrs. Woods struggled to her feet. "Oh, all right, Sylvan. But I really feel strange."

"Let yourselves go," Sylvan explained. "Dance any way you like. Give in to the music."

"I never play for 'attack' before," said Penko. "What I play?"

"Ruchenitza! Play Ruchenitza!"

The priests and monks smiled and whispered among themselves when they heard the word "Ruchenitza."

Penko started playing *Svatbarska Ruchenitza*—the dance Sylvan had heard at the wedding in Asenovgrad.

"Relax, everybody. Move your feet like this: Quick, quick, slow; quick, quick, slow." Sylvan danced to demonstrate. "Come on, try it!"

A priest began dancing; some monks joined him. Then Dr. Lume jumped on the dance floor. He tapped his feet, waved his arms, and gazed heavenward, crying, "Beethoven! Beethoven!"

"Looks like Lume is having an attack right now," Sam observed.

Ludo stood before the dancing priest, and towering over him, bobbed his head up and down, made grotesque faces, and tried stamping his feet on the priest's long black robe.

"Don't go after the priest," Sylvan coached. "Go after the *feeling*." He pointed to his heart. "In here!"

"Gotcha," Ludo shouted, and immediately turned from the priest, jumped on the refectory table, and danced a bouncy step like a ping-pong ball in perfect timing to the music.

Lilyana pulled Mrs. Woods to the center of the floor. "Come, Mother Sylvan, dance!"

"But I only know the fox trot."

Lilyana showed her a step. Mrs. Woods' feet moved like a pigeon; the flesh under her arms wiggled. "*I feel* it," Mrs. Woods cried, repeating the step over and over again. "I feel something under my feet!"

"Get off my toe!" snapped Schlossberger, whose movements had nothing to do with the music or rhythm of the dance. Rather, they consisted of a series of facial ticks, lurches, and convulsive spasms. His huge feet pounded the floor. The priests, thinking he was doing an imitation of the American president, cheered him on.

Penko changed keys on his gaida, and speeded up the tempo. Shouts of "*Dai go zhivo!*" and "Hi, ha!" rose from the monks.

Vladimir Gussman stood to the side, aloof from the dance. "This is silly," he muttered to Sam. "Would you participate in such a thing?"

"I would," said Sam, "but only with *you.*" He grabbed the conductor by the arm. "Come!" he commanded, dragging him onto the dance floor. Sam threw his shirt on a bench, then danced a step combining the Tango with a *pas de bourree* from Tchaikovsky's Swan Lake. Beads of sweat shone on his forehead as he shouted, "Eeeyaaa!" and tried playing Tartini's Devil's Trill Sonata on Gussman's nose. "Come on, Vladi. Let's see your *attack!*"

"Get your fingers off my face!" Gussman wheezed, pulling a baton out of his vest pocket. "Luckily, I like Tchaikovsky." Maintaining a most dignified expression, he conducted while Penko played Ruchenitza. Then he went over to the other dancers to personally conduct their dancing. Everyone liked it except Mr. Woods, who tore the baton out of his hand and grabbed him around the waist. Soon, they did a rumba together.

"Stop this immediately!" Gussman protested. "Give me back my baton!"

Mr. Woods was firm. "Shut up and *dance!*"

Once again, Penko changed keys; the tempo increased. More shouts of "*Dai go zhivo!*", "Brr!", "*Asega!*" and "Hi, ha!" filled the room.

Sylvan saw one of the priests leaving. Soon, he returned carrying a *tupan*—the large Bulgarian drum. A monk started playing a *gadulka*—a Bulgarian fiddle. Penko welcomed both of them without missing a beat. As the volume of sound increased, so did the energy of the dancers.

Sylvan spied bottles of sliva on the table. Where did they come from? A miracle from heaven? Or did the monastery have an underground bottling plant?

Linda downed a glass, then danced opposite Schlossberger, who shouted out stock market quotations.

The sun set; the moon rose; evening turned into midnight. Americans and Bulgarians toasted to eternal friendship, embraced, and handed out addresses and phone numbers. Gussman herded Sam, Ludo, Mr. and Mrs. Woods, and Schlossberger together to sing a chorus of "For He's A Jolly Good Fellow." Schlossberger collapsed after the fifteenth chorus, but was revived by Dr. Lume, who whispered tales of secret silver futures in his ear. Then Lume fell on his knees, thanking God that Beethoven was Bulgarian, and recited poems by Shelley and Keats that he had translated into Yiddish.

The monks clapped and cheered. Three of them removed the large picture of Lenin from the refectory wall and presented it to Mr. and Mrs. Woods as a gift.

"Friend Amerikanski!" a young priest cried, whisking an icon off the shelf and sticking it into Sam's pocket. Moved deeply, Sam gave the priest a piece of bubble gum and his Exxon credit card, saying "That's all you need to get by in America."

By 3:00 a.m., Penko was still playing his gaida while Ludo danced. Dr. Lume and Mr. Woods had fallen asleep on top of each other. Schlossberger dozed in the corner.

At 6:00 A.M., Sylvan trudged up the stairs; he fell into bed, totally exhausted. Soon, he would be going back to the Bronx. He wanted to be well rested for the trip.

.